Dying For Wine (Seeing Red)
(A Tucson Valley Retirement Community Cozy Mystery)
By: Marcy Blesy

This book is a work of fiction. Names, characters, places, and events are a result of the imagination of the author or are used fictitiously. Any resemblance to actual persons, living or dead, businesses, events, or locations is a coincidence.

No part of the text may be reproduced without the written permission of the author, except for brief passages in reviews.

Copyright © 2023 by Marcy Blesy, LLC. All rights reserved. Cover design by Cormar Covers

Chapter 1

"You're off key! Can't you hear yourself?" screams Sherman Padowski, his toupee moving back and forth as he shakes his fist in anger.

Clyde Andrews, the target of his rage, rolls his eyes in irritation at the man who looks a lot like him save for the toupee on Sherman's head. Clyde has his own hair combed neatly and greased back in the vein of a 1960s Filly Sinclair hairstyle. And since they are both Filly Sinclair impersonators, it makes sense that they'd bear a resemblance. With or without the toupee, both men are undeniably still handsome.

"Can't you go down an octave?" asks Sherman, frustrated that he's having to give singing advice to someone that makes a living singing, like himself.

It's time to step in. My new job encompasses way more than doing the marketing and social media for Tucson Valley Retirement Community. I can't be angry, though. Is anyone ever completely honest when it comes to listing the job responsibilities of an open position? There is usually a reason why the position became available to begin with, and it's not always because a completely satisfied employee married the woman of his dreams and had to leave his beloved job. Sometimes there are unfortunate responsibilities that nobody tells you about. And breaking up disputes between the headliners in the 1960s send-off spring concert at the performing arts center is one of those non-disclosed responsibilities.

"Guys! Stop it. You are both professionals," I remind them. "Can't you work out another way to solve your dispute? Maybe sing another song where you are both happy with the octave?" I'd only agreed to having two Sinclair impersonators because Brenda threw such a stink. It turns out that Sherman Padowski is her cousin's wife's brother, and if we didn't let him sing in the 1960s spring extravaganza, then she was boycotting the event and taking all of her friends and their money with her, too. And as much as I despise the plastic woman with a permanent scowl, this event isn't just an entertainment concert. It's a fundraiser for the performing arts center. We need this event to be a success in order to be able to offer more programs year-round.

"Rosi!"

I turn toward the woman that is yelling my name, but she's only trying to get my attention with her booming voice. She's a harmless soul. "I'm coming, Tracy!"

"There you are, Rosi. I need a final count for the concert attendees. There's a waiting list, and I need to know if there are any cancellations I can give away to those waiting. This has never happened before. We've never had a waiting list. I hate to turn people away because it's like throwing guaranteed money out the window, but we only have so many seats. Your marketing campaign has been brilliant, Rosi, just brilliant. How you got JJ McMeadows to emcee our concert was a stroke of genius. The amount of lusting the women in my tap dance class have expressed over that man would curl your toes. If you could hear the things they've said. Hmmm. Hmm! And I'm the baby in the class at 55." She laughs, a pleasing belly laugh that endears her to anyone who crosses her path.

Tracy is the best boss I have ever worked for. I know it's not politically correct to have worried about working for a female boss, but all of my other bosses had been male. And even though the last one fired me from the Springfield Gazette, I really couldn't hold it against him because he'd learned about the tires I'd slashed on my then-husband's mistress's car. He'd been a good boss, though, and gave me a lot of latitude to cover stories the way I wanted to tell them in Illinois's capital city. But Tracy tops even that boss. She's kind and personable. And trusting.

She's unorganized and forgetful, too. That makes me the perfect addition to the team, as she refers to us. She leads with the glowing personality, and I finish with the organization and details. We have a great lineup of shows and events planned, but this concert will be a farewell event of sorts for the snowbirds who will leave Arizona for the summer and go back to their homes spread out around the country. Mom and Dad are going back to Illinois soon, too.

"I'll check my messages, but I don't know of any cancellations. Maybe we can add a row of seats in the back of the auditorium behind the row of stadium seats. I think that would allow eight or ten more spots. What do you think?"

"Have Mario take some chairs from the conference room into the auditorium and guesstimate how many would fit comfortably. And check the fire code to make sure we won't be overcapacity if we add seats. The last thing we need is for this show to be shut down because of a fire code violation. Oh me, oh my, the women in this community would never forgive me! Or, the men, either, for that matter. There are just as many men geeking out over JJ McMeadows's upcoming appearance.

"Dance craze. It's a dance craze, baby. Follow me on the dance floor." Tracy sings aloud as she twirls around the auditorium to JJ McMeadows's 1967 hit single. Neither of us were alive then, but the song is catchy, and several of the people I've run into since the announcement of JJ's participation in our event have shared their personal stories of seeing JJ perform when they were in their teens. They always have smiles on their faces when they tell their stories. Karen, my favorite of Mom's gaggle of gossipy friends, was blushing as she told me about having a first date with her future husband Albert when he kissed her on the lips as JJ sang "Teenage Lover." Karen and Albert had been married for fifty years before he died three years ago. Now she's "enjoying time" with Bob Horace, as she puts it. And I'm hoping that even though the concert may be bittersweet for her, she can find joy again.

"Forward me the information about the waiting list. I'll take care of that issue. You've got other things to attend to. I hear the lines at the new pickleball court were painted incorrectly."

Tracy rolls her eyes. "You have no idea what a mess those new courts have been. A three-inch discrepancy has driven the die-hards mad."

I stifle a giggle.

"Thanks. I'll take you up on your offer. You're a godsend, Rosi, an absolute godsend. There are too many balls in the air for one person to manage the social activities at all of our facilities here in Tucson Valley. I'm grateful that the board *finally* agreed to let me hire another person after Teddy left six months ago. It's been a nightmare keeping the swimmers and the pickleballers and the artists and the actors and the card players and the…"

I put a hand on Tracy's arm. She's spiraling. "Get a fresh coffee. I've got this."

She nods her head, takes a deep breath, and spins down the hallway as she sings "Dance Craze" to herself on the way back to her office.

Back in my office, I settle at my desk which overlooks the parking lot of the Tucson Valley Retirement Community. It's not a glamorous office with an amazing view, but it beats the cold days of early spring I'd be experiencing back in Illinois. I try not to dwell on what Arizona summers may be like. Barley, my new puppy, jumps onto my lap to interrupt my thoughts. She's getting big quickly, and her Golden Retriever features grow more beautiful every day, even the fur that's constantly flying around her. She's the best thing that's happened to me since my trip to Tucson. It's still hard to admit to myself that my trip to help my parents after Dad's knee replacement surgery has turned into a new permanent residence, a new puppy, and a budding friendship with a hot landscaper. Life after divorce isn't so bad after all. Moving on sounds cliché, but it's truly the best medicine for a broken heart. It doesn't just mean moving on with a new relationship but being willing to try new things. And no one can claim that I haven't tried new things. As if on cue, my office phone rings.

"Hello, this is Rosi Laruee. How may I help you?"

"Hi, Rosi. It's me. Jan."

Barf is what I want to say to my mother's other snooty friend, Jan Jinkins. She and Brenda are two peas in a shriveled-up pod. "Hello, Jan. How may I help you?"

"I'm calling to check on that wait list. Frank and I have tickets, of course, but my sister and brother-in-law, Allen's parents," she says with emphasis as if I could forget her loathsome nephew who'd made a laughingstock of me at karaoke night when he'd visited his beloved aunt. "are extending their visit to see JJ McMeadows, and they just *have* to get tickets."

"It is going to be a great night."

"You don't seem to understand, Rosi. They *have* to get tickets. I promised Mary Lou I'd get her those tickets."

"We will do our best to accommodate everyone that wants to attend the concert, Jan. However, we only have so many—"

"Get me those tickets, Rosi. Get me those tickets."

The phone line goes dead.

"Well then, Barley. Perhaps I should check on that waiting list," I sigh. Tracy's agreement to allow me to bring Barley to the office was icing on the cake to an amazing job package. Barley has a way of lowering the temperature of everyone in the office, especially when they have to deal with entitled narcissists like Jan who think that the world should revolve around them. I'd finally asked Mom why she'd chosen Jan and Brenda as friends. "It just kind of happened, Rosi," she'd said. "They came from central Illinois, too, and there is a large contingency of Illinoisians here. I know it's silly, but people tend to form their social groups based upon geography." It made sense to me that the beginnings of relationships might start out that way, but the fact that they *stayed* that way simply because of the state someone had come from seemed pitiful. But I didn't tell Mom that, of course.

I open my computer to check my emails. Tracy's updated list has four names of people wanting tickets, not including Allen's parents. No messages of cancellation have come in to me, but two new requests for tickets have arrived, from Sparrow and her wife Tina. Sparrow said she'd be in town to finish the sale of her sister's store and saw the notice about the concert and could I see about getting her tickets? That's a request I am willing to try harder to fill than Allen's parents. I'm so glad that Salem's Stories has a buyer. It'd be a shame to see such a fine bookstore close its doors for good. And now that Salem's murder has been solved, the eeriness of her murder in her own store holds much less fear.

Barley jumps off my lap and starts barking at the window. I turn around to see Keaton walking through the parking lot to the building. Sometimes I think that Barley loves Keats more than she loves me.

Barley paws at my office door, anticipating Keaton's lunchtime arrival, a new routine we've established:

Wednesday lunches together. I pull out a compact mirror from my purse, run my fingers through my long brown hair, and reapply lip gloss so I look casually put together while trying hard not to look like I'm trying hard.

Keaton's face lights up when he sees Barley. His work pants are lightly dirty, but he's put on a clean shirt, I observe, while he squats down to greet Barley. "Hey, girl! How has your day been? The boss treating you okay?" He flashes a smile at me before reaching into his pocket and giving Barley a treat. She licks his hand affectionately. He stands up and walks toward me where I am standing, awaiting his attention next. "Sorry! I didn't bring you a treat!" he laughs.

"Honestly, just seeing you today is treat enough." I accept his kiss. "But don't let that go to your head! I've had some difficult customers today," I say, reaching for my purse. "Can we take Barley and get our food to go? She needs a walk."

"Sure. It sounds like you might need some fresh air, too."

"I do!" I wave goodbye to Tracy in her office and pass by the open door of the auditorium where we are greeted with shouting.

"Clyde, you fool! You're going to screw this whole concert up!"

I peek inside to see Sherman yelling at Clyde. Clyde is standing center stage with a microphone in his shaking hand.

"Do you need to deal with that?" Keaton asks as we spy on the Filly Sinclairs.

"Nope. It can wait. I've discovered that settling disputes between two stubborn, old men isn't a task I'm designed to handle well, *especially* on an empty stomach. Come on. Let's go."

Chapter 2

"Tell me about your day," I say as we eat our sandwiches on a blanket Keaton has pulled from his truck and put down in Tuttle Park, away from the pickleball action. Barley snores nearby under the shade of a small hopseed bush. I do miss the shade of a good old Midwestern maple tree.

"Well," Keaton stretches his arms above his head. "Today is all about watering. We've been planting a lot of annuals in the past few weeks. Now it's maintenance time. We're in a desert, and water is a commodity not to be taken for granted."

"Why bother when it's going to be so hot soon?"

Keaton shrugs his shoulders. "Flowers make people happy, and rich people have money to spend to keep their community looking nice. Do you think it's a waste?" He tucks a piece of my hair behind my ear. His touch makes me shiver involuntarily.

"No, of course not. I love flowers like the next guy. There's just such a disparity in this world between how the rich live and how the homeless people in the large towns in southern Arizona are living."

Keaton nods his head. "You're right about that. If you can solve that problem, enlighten me."

I laugh. "I can't even solve the problems between two Sinclair impersonators or find enough seats for all the people that want to see JJ McMeadows in person. I don't think I can take on the homeless issue today, too."

"Well, if anyone can solve those problems, it's Rosi Laruee." He smiles and stares at me as if trying to read my thoughts.

"Your confidence delights me."

Barley's barking startles us both. A woman with a tight bun that matches her taut face is walking toward us in a huff, her small white poodle following closely behind. Barley wags her tail, hoping for a playmate, but Ralphie is not the kind of dog who plays. He's a show dog with an attitude. "Hello, Brenda," I say to the woman who is nearly breathless when she reaches us. A sweatshirt is tied around her waist, and her green tank top shows sweat marks under her breasts. I've never seen her looking so un-put together.

"Rosi Laruee! I have been looking for you all over this god-forsaken park. Why can't you be in one of the pavilions like a normal person who has a picnic lunch?" she asks, waving her hand over the blanket we are sitting on.

Keaton pulls Barley closer but doesn't say a word. He leaves Brenda to me.

"What's the matter, Brenda?" I put a grape in my mouth, so she sees how unbothered by her that I am, though I am very much bothered by her interruption to my lunch date with Keaton.

"Sherman just called me."

"That's nice." I take another grape.

"He says that Clyde Andrews is being a skunk and that you won't do anything about it."

I raise an eyebrow. *A skunk?* "They are grown men, Brenda. Certainly they can solve any differences they may have about artistic choices. The show promises to highlight many different voices with music from the '60s, and the fact that we have not one—but *two*—Sinclair-type singers will only add to the flavor of the show. Of course," I pause, as I squint up at Brenda, the sun shining brightly from over her shoulder, "if Sherman is so unhappy, he's welcome to take his talent elsewhere."

Brenda audibly gasps, pulling on Ralphie's lead so that he goes tumbling backwards toward her with a whimper. It's the first time I've ever felt sorry for the mangy rat.

"Sherman is a five-time Filly Sinclair impersonator winner in Allen County, Indiana. That's unprecedented!" Her wild eyes match those of Ralphie who seems very confused by his owner's demeanor.

"Unprecedented," I repeat sarcastically.

Brenda ignores me. "Get that Clyde guy under control or else."

"Or else what, Brenda?" Keaton asks for the first time as Brenda hasn't yet acknowledged his presence.

"I have money. I know people. I will tank this concert so fast it will leave your head spinning if you don't make things comfortable for Sherman. He is a good man. He is a most talented man. He is a handso…" She stops talking mid-sentence as if remembering that she isn't talking to her gossip group. She pats the sides of her hair and takes a deep breath. "Please see to it that Sherman's demands—needs—are met." She nods at Keaton and me, tugs on Ralphie's leash again, and storms off across the park. I wish at that moment that she'd fall into a cactus like the one that had befallen me months ago.

Barley barks gruffly at Keaton to be released from his grip. Even the poor dog is in a sour mood. "That was something," he says. "How does Brenda know that guy?"

"Sherman? Apparently, he is her cousin's wife's brother." I shrug my shoulders.

"She acts like he's a personal friend, a close friend—if you know what I mean."

"You got that vibe, too? The ironic thing is that it's *Sherman* who is the overbearing troublemaker, not Clyde. He's way too docile. Ugh. I have to get back to work. There is so much to do before Saturday's show."

"When does the rest of the entertainment arrive?" Keaton asks as he folds the blanket.

"The Sinclair guys are here already, clearly. The Martha Franklin and Tommy Davis Jr. impersonators arrive tonight. The Denny Martino and Star impersonators fly in tomorrow before rehearsals."

"No Sunny Moon?"

"Oh, yeah, Xander lives locally. He'll be at rehearsals."

"That's quite a lineup—a wide variation from the 1960s, I mean."

"Yep. There's never been a lineup with this combination before. It's part of the appeal of the show—that, and my amazing marketing ability, of course."

"Of course," says Keaton as he grabs my waist and pulls me close, kissing me on the lips. "Have a great rest of your day. Are we still on for condo hunting tonight?"

"I completely forgot about that!" I can feel beads of sweat roll down the back of my neck. How am I going to survive living in Arizona in July when I'm already suffering in April?

"I'm sure you can cancel with the realtor. And…the offer to stay with me still stands." He smiles devilishly.

I shake my head back and forth. "It's a tempting offer. I need to get out of my parents' place before they go back to Illinois and the owner returns, but I think I'd better stick to a solo living arrangement for now."

"Just remember that the offer stands." He kisses me again, pats Barley on her head, and I follow him to his truck. Despite Brenda literally running into our picnic, I've been reminded how easy it is to be with Keaton. But it is way too early to live with someone again. My divorce has only been final for a year.

"Thanks for the lunch," I say, as Barley and I jump out of Keaton's truck at the performing arts center. "I'll meet you after work at the Javelina Drive address I sent you. I don't want to cancel the appointment."

"Sounds good. Let me know if you change your mind. Good luck with the Sinclair boys." He winks as I close the door.

"Come on, Barley. We can do this." I march confidently back into the senior center with Barley at my heels.

Chapter 3

"*Fly me to...*" the melodious sounds of a Filly Sinclair song flow from the auditorium into the hallway as I walk to my office in the adjoining senior center. That's a hopeful sign that Sherman and Clyde figured out who'd be singing what part or at least who was singing what song. I mean, for goodness' sake, it's not even a Sinclair-highlighting show. It's a '60s themed musical night covering the music of many different artists.

"Oh, there you are, Rosi," says Mario who is pushing a cart full of chairs toward the auditorium. "Want to see what these chairs look like in the back? I tested a couple and think we might be able to get eight additional seats if we aren't violating the fire code."

"Fire code isn't a problem as long as we have more than twenty-four inches between the rows. The room is approved for 850 people including performers and with eight additional seats, we'd be right around 775. Let's take a look."

I help Mario set up the additional chairs at the back of the auditorium. While it's not ideal to use office chairs for guests when all of the other attendees will be sitting in plush seats, it's better than nothing. I would have sat on a beanbag for a chance to see NYSNC back in the day! "Thanks, Mario. Everything looks great in here. The auditorium is spotless, and the extra seating is very much appreciated."

Mario beams when complimented. I don't think he gets complimented often. He always looks so sad at the end of the day when he leaves to go home. Mom told me that Paula had told Karen who'd told her that Mario's wife is a lazy grump who yells as him all the time, but that's just what the gossip brigade says. She sent muffins to work with Mario the week I started, and I thought that was really thoughtful.

"You're welcome, Rosi. Anything else I can do before I leave for the day?" he asks expectantly, as if wishing for me to say yes.

"Actually, there is," I say more seriously than I'd intended.

"Sure! Name it!" His eyes light up.

"JJ McMeadows's assistant has sent a very specific list of items she'd like to be available for JJ when he arrives tomorrow."

"Ah, a diva," he says, shaking his head back and forth.

"Yes, something like that," I laugh. I pull out my phone to read through the list again on the text message I'd receive from JJ's assistant Dee. "Do you have any idea where I might find manuka honey?" I wrinkle my nose in confusion as I read the list aloud. "And lavender-scented candles—two of them. I need two of them."

"Oh, wow. Have the others made demands, too?" He strokes his graying beard.

"Not anything unusual that I know of, but I'm going to go over my emails again. The Celtic dancers were a piece of cake for my first program at the performing arts center last month. They came in, danced, got on the bus, and drove away. We barely knew they were here except for the two hours they were performing."

"Well…" says Mario. "I knew they were here. I'm still buffing out the floor behind the stage they used for practice in those fancy shoes."

I laugh. "Your efforts are very much appreciated. So, do you think you can figure out where to find that special honey?"

"I'll call Celia. If there is any manuka honey in Tucson Valley, she'll find it."

"Thanks, Mario."

My office phone is blinking, a reminder that updating our technology should really be a priority. I push the voicemail button and listen to the message.

"Hello," says a man with a deep voice that could both talk me to sleep and mesmerize me at the same time. *"This is JJ McMeadows. I was hoping to talk with a Rosi Laruee. My assistant has, well, has moved on, shall I say? I need to make sure a few things are in order before my arrival in Tucson Valley tomorrow."*

I reluctantly return JJ's call. "Absolutely, Mr. McMeadows," I say after he repeats his entire message as if I hadn't just listened to it. "We are very excited about your arrival. We've even been able to add a few more seats for the show."

"That's fantastic. There were 15,000 people at my last performance."

"Oh, well, that's great. But we have seats for 775."

"It's a charity event for me in Tucson Valley. I'm the emcee. It's quite a difference from the crowds I usually command, however."

"Of course. What can I help you with today, Mr. McMeadows?"

"Call me JJ. Mr. McMeadows is my father, and he's 99."

"Yes, JJ. And please call me Rosi. What can I do for you?"

"I am hoping this conversation can be discrete."

"I can do my best."

"Your best isn't enough." His words fall hard through the phone line. "I need you to keep this request confidential."

"Okay." What is supposed to be a fun, send-off concert of sorts before the snowbirds return to their homes for the spring and summer is turning into a drama-filled event.

"Elena's dressing room must be placed next to mine. No exceptions."

"Who?"

"Star!" he says in frustration. "Elena Templeton impersonates Star. And her dressing room must be adjoining mine."

"Mr. Mc…JJ, we are a simple organization. We don't have dressing rooms for each of the performers. There is essentially a men and women's changing area."

"Balderdash!" he yells through the phone.

"Excuse me?" I scrunch up my face as Tracy pokes her head into my office.

"I've never performed without a private dressing room."

"As you yourself mentioned, this is a fundraising event. I'm sure you can understand that."

"That won't do. I won't come if I don't have a private dressing room. And Elena needs a room adjoining mine. If that cannot be accommodated, I will cancel your little 'fundraising' event, Ms. Laruee. Good day."

The phone line goes dead. I stare at the phone, wondering for the tenth time in the last week why I decided to take this job and leave the newspaper industry. The fact that I was fired from my job and that few people even read newspapers anymore is not lost on me, but this job isn't a walk in the park. It's more like a walk in the park where you trip over a cactus and get spines stuck in your hands. I look at my palms where I still have tiny scars from doing that very thing.

"What was that all about?" asks Tracy. She's holding a stack of file folders, another reminder that we need to update our technology. I've never worked for someone that uses so many file folders. She appears organized on the outside, but all it takes is for one file folder to be stuck inside another to throw off the whole system, not to mention a trip and fall while holding a stack like Tracy is doing right now.

"I'm not supposed to say." I roll my eyes. "But I have no idea how to fulfill this diva's demands without your help."

"Let's talk. I was going to ask for your help planning for the summer series." She points to the file folders. "But it seems we have a bit more work to do first."

"Thanks." I rub my temples and lean my elbows on the desk. Tracy sits across from me. I take a deep breath. "JJ McMeadows is threatening to cancel."

Her eyes go wide. "Why?"

"He's demanding a private dressing room."

Tracy grins. "And why does he even need to 'dress?' He's just the announcer."

"I know, but there's more."

Tracy raises her eyebrows. "More? Do tell," she says slyly.

"He's demanding a private dressing room for Elena Templeton, too."

"Who's that?" she asks.

"Star."

"As in Sunny and Star?"

"The very one or one of dozens, I imagine. She's a popular artist for impersonators."

"Does he know her?"

"I have no idea. If he doesn't know her, I imagine he wishes he did. Why else would he want an adjoining dressing room?"

"What are you going to do?"

"I was hoping you would tell me what to do. You're my boss."

Tracy laughs. "I am the executive director of the Tucson Valley Retirement Community Senior Center. It's my job to oversee the daily programs and special events, to budget, to keep our residents happy. It's also my job to hire smart people like you to figure out the details that make things run smoothly. This is your problem, Rosi. Whatever you decide, you have my support, as long as JJ McMeadows shows up tomorrow with his demands met."

"But if I give them private dressing rooms, then everyone will want that."

"Yep. Talk with Mario. You'll figure it out. I have a meeting with the aquatic director. Apparently, there's a leakage problem in the pool."

"That's too bad. I imagine it costs a lot of money to fill the pool."

"Not that kind of leakage, Rosi. Not that kind of leakage." She shakes her head back and forth as she's walking out of my office. "You have my blessing! But figure it out soon!"

Chapter 4

I text the realtor to reschedule my condo and apartment hunting until Monday. There is simply too much going on this week to concentrate on my next home. Plus, Mom and Dad have three more weeks before they head back to Illinois, so it's not like I don't have a place to stay although I'd hoped to be out of their home before my brother arrived. I'll be relegated to the couch as Simon and his wife Shelly will take over the bedroom with their toddler sons Flynn and Hudson, 4 and 3 respectively, and brand-new baby Ivy. Mom is over the moon about their visit. It had been delayed because Shelly didn't want to travel with a tiny baby. I don't blame her, of course. I also wouldn't want to drive with two toddlers, but Simon is the golden son, and there hasn't been a year when Mom and Dad have been in Tucson that he hasn't visited even though they'll see each other in a few weeks as Simon and Shelly only live a half hour from them. If it were me, I would have waited. That's a lot of stress on a family. But I'm not the one making the decisions. Anyway, that will be next week's problem. Simon is coming—with his perfect family and children. One problem at a time. Super yeah!

How's your afternoon?

A text from Keaton brightens my mood.

Getting worse. Cancelled realtor appointment. Will be working late.

How about I stop by for a drink later?

Sounds good. Dad loves his beer drinking buddy.

Ha! He's cool. But I love my wine drinking buddy.

Love? That's the first time Keaton has used that word, even in a text. Was it a slip? Again, I don't have time to ponder my new relationship. My new job takes precedence. I metaphorically roll up my sleeves to get to work. I am smart. Tracy is right. I can do this. I write out the names of each of the performers.

    JJ McMeadows: Master of Ceremonies

    Sherman Padowski: Filly Sinclair 1

    Clyde Andrews: Filly Sinclair 2

    Kenny Davis: Tommy Davis Jr.

    Douggy Carson: Denny Martino

    Elena Templeton: Star

    Xander Nolan: Sunny Moon

    Nancy Ontario: Martha Franklin

I stare at the list. It's really an impressive group of impersonators. This show has great potential to raise a lot of money. Not only does the money from the tickets go to the senior center, but guests are being asked to make further donations at their discretion when they leave the show, kind of like a tip for a bartender or an offering at church. And I've managed to secure so many advertisers for the program that the allocated fund for paying the performers can remain almost intact. It helps that the performers are also giving us a discount. Tucson Valley holds the status as being one of the finest retirement communities in the Southwest. Performing here boosts anyone's cred and ability to get future gigs.

That makes seven performers plus the emcee, the major complainer being JJ McMeadows, although he'd give Sherman Padowski a run for his money in a head-to-head battle for alpha male. I pull out the map of the senior center and attached performing arts auditorium. There are two backstage rooms that serve as staging areas for any acts that may need the space. There's a fresh set of claw marks behind the door of the room closest to the stage from the dancing dogs that performed in February, right before I arrived in Tucson Valley to help my parents after Dad's knee replacement surgery. Neither room is decked out for superstars. Superstars don't usually perform here. And no *real* superstars are performing here again this weekend, save for JJ McMeadows, and he hasn't been a top 100 chart maker for decades. I sigh. This job was supposed to be a relaxing change from chasing news stories around the Illinois capital. I stare at the map again. "If I clear out the storage rooms, I might be able to make four dressing rooms, but Elena and Nancy will have to share a room. And if JJ has the room next door, then I can split the other men up into…"

"Excuse me, Rosi?"

I look up from my desk. "Oh, hi, Mario."

He looks around the room. "Are you talking to someone?" he asks. "I thought I heard someone talking."

I laugh. "I'm talking to myself. It helps me to sort out some of the issues with the show this weekend."

"More problems?" he asks.

"More problems."

"I hope this will help." Mario holds up a large jar, like something you'd find at Costco or
Sam's Club, whatever it contains meant to last for years.

"What's that?"

"Manuka honey," he says. "Celia had some in our pantry," he beams. "I knew she'd find some." He seems proud, and I can tell he really cares for her no matter the gossip.

"You're the best! Please thank her for me. I take the honey and set it on the bookshelf behind me next to the lavender candle I already owned, my favorite scent for relaxation. I don't have two candles, like JJ's assistant asked for, but since she's no longer involved for whatever reason, one candle will have to do. "I have another big ask, Mario. I need help cleaning out the two storage rooms backstage. I need the additional space for our performers."

"Let me guess. Someone thinks they need their own room."

"You guessed it."

"Same pain in the butt?"

"Yep. JJ."

Mario shakes his head. "Why do people have to be like that?"

"I don't know, but he's threatening to cancel which Tracy says can't happen, so if you'll help me figure out where to move all the junk—I mean, stuff—then I'll stay as late as need be to move it there."

"Let me look around. Meet me onstage in ten minutes. I'll have it figured out by then."

"Thanks, Mario."

I send emails to Sparrow and Tammy letting them know they have tickets for Saturday's show.

I consider skipping over Allen's parents on the waiting list under Jan's name, but they are the next names on the list, so I send an email to Jan, too. At least she should get off Mom's back for a bit since her daughter did her a favor.

A knock at my door startles me. I look up from my computer. Barley looks up from her dog bed where she'd been sleeping. Clyde Andrews has changed out of his suit, which he'd insisted he needed to wear today to get into the role of playing Mr. Sinclair. The wrinkles on his face look deeper close up, and he looks tired. "Ms. Laruee, I have a favor to ask."

Here we go again. "What can I do for you, Mr. Andrews?"

"As you know, Sherman has some strong opinions about my singing ability. I'd like to remind you that I was the first Filly Sinclair impersonator asked to perform in Tucson Valley. There wasn't even supposed to be another

Sinclair performer until someone with connections convinced you to allow two of us to perform."

I sigh. "Yes, Mr. Andrews, I'm really sorry about that. Politics are at play everywhere nowadays. But I'm happy to hear that you've worked everything out. You sound amazing," I exaggerate as I'm really only hoping they sound great because I truly don't know what they've been doing during the last couple of hours of practice.

"I don't feel safe, Ms. Laruee."

"What do you mean?"

"Sherman threatened me."

I wrinkle my forehead. "Can you elaborate, please?"

"He's a very intimidating man. There's something that's off with him. He has an unusual temper."

"I'm sorry that he's causing issues. Perhaps you should keep your distance until the concert. Do you think that might help? We have some lovely hotel rooms reserved for you. Maybe a little distance would be good for you both?" I feel like I'm refereeing a dispute between Zak and his best friend when they went through a spell when they were nine and all they did was argue. Turns out it was a spot at first base on their little league team that caused their consternation.

"I suppose that will be nice. But keep your eye on that guy. He's a troublemaker."

"Will do, Mr. Andrews. Have a wonderful night. I look forward to seeing you tomorrow afternoon when the other performers have arrived for rehearsal. Until then, enjoy the community, and keep some distance between you and Mr. Padowski."

He smiles slightly, a deep blue eye color on display, Ol' Mr. Blue Eyes. "Have a good day, Ms. Laruee."

"You as well."

I let my breath out slowly. "Come on, Barley, let's move some junk." Barley follows me out of my office, wagging her tail excitedly.

Mario and I spend the next hour moving assorted items from the storage rooms into old cabinet areas under the stage. Tracy pitches in when she doesn't find me in my office. We carry an assortment of items that include easels, large pads of paper, old props from past performances, a plastic palm tree, bags of yarn from a former yarn demonstration. The old cabinets are really only cobweb-covered spaces under the stage. No one save a toddler could even stand inside. I am a sweaty mess. But when the storage rooms are cleared, I am satisfied with our work. I place JJ McMeadows's manuka honey jar and lavender candle in one of the four rooms along with a name tag I made on my computer. Next to his room, I place a name tag marked as Martha Franklin and Star. I think Elena and Nancy will like that. I place the men in the former storage rooms: Filly Sinclair 1 (Sherman) with Tommy Davis Jr. (Kenny) in one room and Filly Sinclair 2 (Clyde) with Denny Martino (Douggy) and Sunny Moon (Xander). Tomorrow I will touch base with all the performers after they have arrived and make sure they're set up for rehearsal before the evening's show. I'm on top of this event now. All in a day's work.

Chapter 5

I'd tried to cancel my date with Keaton at my parents' last night because I knew I was a bit grumpy, but he'd come by anyway at 9:00 with a bottle of wine. I'd already put on my overnight face mask and looked like a clown in white paint, but he didn't care. We drank wine on the backyard patio and tried to identify constellations in the clear night sky. It was nice. It was easy. Nothing about today is going to be easy. That is abundantly clear when I see that my clunker of an office phone is flashing with not one but four messages. I enter the passcode, grab a pen and paper for notes, and take a deep breath.

"This is Douggy Carson. My plane from San Diego is delayed. I need my driver to arrive at 3:30 now. Thanks."

"Hi. Just reminding you that I need manuka honey in my dressing room. Don't want you to think that just because my assistant is no longer with me that I don't expect my wishes to be attended to. This is JJ."

"Hello. My name is Elena Templeton. I'm the Star impersonator. My plane from Phoenix has been delayed. Could you please let me know if transportation can pick me up around 3:30 now so that I can attend rehearsals? Thank you. I am very excited for the show!"

"Hi, Rosi. This is Brenda. Sherman is still very unhappy with how he is being treated by Clyde. Please take care of this problem."

I collapse into my chair. Every day this week brings a headache before 9:00. It will all be over in 12 hours I remind myself. I pick up my cellphone and push the call button. "Hey, Dad. Change of plans. Can you pick Douggy Carson and Elena Templeton up at 3:30 now instead of 2:00? It looks like their planes are both delayed, though I don't understand why Elena doesn't just drive from Phoenix. Great. Thanks. I appreciate your help. Yes, tell Mom she can drop off the muffins any time before 4:00. Great. Yes, it will all be great. Of course, the Golden Girls' plastic container will be a huge hit. Bye." One problem solved. It's quite helpful when the transportation department for the show is genetically related.

I do a walkthrough of the new dressing rooms, all four of them now. I made gift baskets of things I'd purchased at Walmart last night after Mario and I were done clearing the rooms. Everyone is getting a bag of M and M's (regular because I don't know if anyone has a peanut allergy), a bag of specialty popcorn from Tucson Tastes, and a Tucson Valley pen. The splurge from the budget was my purchase of bottles of honey wine and wine glasses from a well-known winery in Tucson. The idea had come to me after JJ's silly request for his special jar of honey. I wonder if he'll understand. I doubt it. People like JJ McMeadows are so narcissistic that they don't recognize when they are being mocked. It's more than any performer has ever received, but nothing is normal about this show. Everything is over the top, and I haven't even met most of the performers yet. I set a small matchbook of matches next to JJ's lavender candle on a coffee table in his dressing room along with the gigantic manuka honey jar. The bathrooms are cleaned. The stage has been swept. The local band members and backup singers are arriving an hour before the performers to practice by themselves first. The final song, to which they are providing accompaniment, is the only known song for tonight's show. The rest of the agenda will be set by the performers. But it finally seems like it's coming together.

"Why can't you do anything right? You're an idiot!" I hear a woman's voice shouting at someone.

I walk toward the noise that seems to be coming from the auditorium after a peaceful lunch. I put down Mom's homemade ham and cheese sandwich and fruit. It's nice to have your mom pack your lunch even when you're almost 40.

Brenda, dressed in a leather skirt and heals, and her husband George stand on the stage near a row of microphone stands and a set of drums. Brenda's expression changes the moment she sees me coming up the aisle of the auditorium.

"Rosi! You startled me!" George drops his head and averts my eyes by moving the microphone stands though they'd been placed exactly where they belong.

"Is everything okay?" I ask.

"Everything is fine as long as you've put that Clyde character in his place. George and I are making sure things are set up for the finale. This is quite an honor for those of us chosen to be a part of an historical concert." She smiles though her lips barely move.

I wouldn't go so far as to call this concert historical, but it should be fun. "I think that our Filly Sinclair impersonators are quite capable of settling their differences, Brenda. Thank you for your concern. We are all eagerly anticipating the finale featuring our local talent." It takes a lot of effort to contain my sarcasm.

"Karen! Paula! Finally, you are here! We can practice now."

Karen has an extra pep in her step. She's wearing a long black skirt with a yellow flowy top, an exit from her regular flower prints. I think being with Bob has improved her confidence. Paula wears a denim skirt with cowboy boots, looking '90s era country stylish as always.

"Ladies, you make an impressive looking group of back-up singers."

"Thanks, Rosi," says Karen.

"This will be great fun," says Paula.

Bob walks into the auditorium next, carrying a trumpet case. He and Leo Lestman, the temporary mayor after Troy Kettleman's unfortunate arrest, make up the local band for tonight's finale along with George who plays drums.

"The playlist you sent us, Rosi, was super helpful," says Leo as he opens his guitar case. "I don't think we will need too much practice. We've been getting together every night for weeks now."

"It's been a blast," says Bob. Karen hugs him from his side, and he smiles like a schoolboy who's had his first crush.

"Well, I think it's just been a silly excuse for you all to get together and drink beer," says Brenda. George sits down at the drum set and hides behind the cymbals.

I am glad my parents are a testament to successful marriages because some people in Tucson Valley would make the perfect models for a divorce lawyer's billboard ad, like Brenda and George. *Is your wife condescending and rude? Need a change? Call 1-800-Help-Me-1.*

"Everything coming along okay?" Tracy asks as I'm hiding in my office until the professional entertainers arrive. I'd just finished texting Keaton about my observations of Brenda and George.

"Good. Everything is all set."

Tracy lets out a deep breath. "Great. I knew you could fit all of the pieces together. I'm really glad you agreed to take this job, Rosi. It takes so much off my plate having you here so that I can manage the books and all of the departments under the senior center's umbrella."

"I'm glad I'm here, too, Tracy." I mean what I say, I realize, as I speak the words aloud. "It feels good to be needed and to be able to put out fires when necessary."

"There will be a lot of strong personalities on that stage tonight."

"That is the understatement of the day."

"I'll be back at 4:00. Text me if you need anything. There's an order for the fitness center I need to check on."

"Hey! How did that leakage problem at the aquatic center work out?"

"It's best if you don't know the details." She laughs and waves goodbye as she walks out of my office.

"The performers are arriving," Mario says as I pick up my phone. "Shall I send them to their dressing rooms?"

"I'll be down, Mario. Thanks."

I brush off crumbs from my fitted, black blazer as I look in my office mirror. I reapply a light pink lip gloss, run a brush through my long brown hair, and smile. Dad says my smile is my best feature. I know I'm going to need it tonight. Let's do this!

Chapter 6

Mario wears his Sunday best. I've never seen him wearing anything but jeans and a t-shirt. He looks nice in his khaki pants and blue polo shirt, his beard neatly trimmed. He's talking to a man I presume is the Sunny Moon impersonator, Xander Nolan, judging by his stature and dark hair.

Nancy, aka Martha Franklin, laughs gregariously at something Kenny is saying. Even for rehearsals, she's dressed the part in a sparkly red pantsuit with tassels that move as she talks. I met Kenny last week when he stopped by to introduce himself. Kenny sings Tommy Davis Jr. songs. His introduction was most memorable as he'd entered my office playing a kazoo. His second surprise I'd discovered the unfortunate way when I sat on the Whoopee cushion on my chair—though by that time no one was there to appreciate the joke.

"Hello, everyone!" I say in a booming voice to those that have arrived on time. I wait until they stop talking and look at me. "I'm so glad to have you all in Tucson Valley. This concert promises to be our best show yet. Everyone is quite excited. We have four dressing room spaces available for you. You'll find a welcome basket for each of you in the rooms that are identified with name plaques. If we can gather in 45 minutes as a group to run through tonight's agenda, that would be wonderful. Until then, please feel free to hang out. Get acquainted. Have a snack. There is a table backstage," I say, pointing in the direction of the table mom had set up. "It's full of muffins, cookies, fruit, and drinks provided by the wonderful residents of Tucson Valley Retirement Community."

A collection of loud voices causes all of us to turn toward the doors of the auditorium.

"You're singing second. I'm not budging. You were only brought into this show because my incompetent assistant thought I was booked for this weekend. You should not be rewarded for that. You were second choice."

"Wrong! You were brought on board because you know someone who knows someone."

"Ha! Use whatever excuse you want, but I'm the headliner…"

We all stop to stare as Sherman and Clyde come into the auditorium, seemingly unaware of our presence because Sherman stops talking the minute he sees us. With one final glare at Clyde, he strides up the aisle to shake the hand of Kenny. The two men talk and laugh as if they are old friends. Conversation resumes around me. I walk toward Clyde who walks toward the dressing room which he will share with Douggy Carson and Xander Nolan.

"Clyde!" I call out his name. He turns slowly toward me.

"Yes?"

"I...I was hoping that things had improved with Sherman. It seems he's still being, uh..., difficult?"

"You could say that," he says sadly.

"I heard you sing yesterday. You are quite talented, and you sound a lot like Filly Sinclair. You're here because you sing well. And the crowd is going to love to hear you."

I see his smile for the first time. "Thank you. It means a lot to hear you say that."

At 4:00, everyone amasses on the stage. No one is in their costumes yet, except for Nancy, so it is kind of hard to imagine this assorted group of people looking and sounding like superstars of the 1960s. She wears a floor-length black gown with sparkles that will reflect nicely under the lights tonight. Her makeup is otherworldly in the amount of detail she's taken to "do her face," but she looks beautiful. The only thing missing is her wig. She stands next to Xander who wears a black vest over a white t-shirt with blue jeans. Kenny divides the two Sinclairs—Sherman and Clyde. He looks so tiny between the two men. He keeps pivoting onto his tiptoes in an attempt to look taller. Everyone laughs. The local backup singers, Paula, Brenda, and Karen, stand next to the local musicians George, Bob, and Leo. The only impersonators missing are Elena and Douggy. They should be arriving with Dad any time now as well as JJ McMeadows who'd insisted on the senior center paying for a private driver in a black car. I'd told him he could ride with my dad in a navy blue Honda CRV, or he'd have to hire his own driver. He'd hired his own driver.

"I just want to go over a few things, and then I will let you, the professionals, sort out how your practice will run. The show starts at 7:00. Your fans will begin arriving at 6:15." I let the word *fans* hang in the air for a second as I watch the faces of everyone light up. "You should be dressed and ready to go before then as we don't want any sneak peeks before your big reveals. Sandwiches will be added to the food table in the back within the hour so when you are done here, please feel free to help yourself to a light dinner. Most of the items have been provided by residents of Tucson Valley Retirement Community, so I think you will find a nice offering of food. After the show, you are welcome to take pictures with the audience members if you choose to or you are free to go."

"When do we receive our money?" asks Sherman Padowski.

"What's the matter, Sherman? Is this your only gig? Hurting for money?" JJ McMeadows has entered the auditorium and shares a smirk with Clyde over the slam.

Sherman glares at JJ, a look that holds deeper meaning than one between two men that have only just met. Sherman doesn't answer as everyone turns toward the back of the auditorium where a woman with long black hair and a bustier that shows ample assets is laughing with a man who's had one too many donuts for breakfast but the sweetest laugh across the cavernous room. They stop talking when they realize they are being watched.

"Hello, everyone!" says the woman. She has the straightest front teeth I have ever seen and also the coolest platform shoes.

"Elena?" I ask.

She nods her head.

I reach out my hand. "Hello. I'm Rosi Laruee. We've spoken on the phone. It's so nice to meet you. I hope that my dad was an acceptable chauffeur.

"Richard is your dad?" she asks, her smile growing. "He was delightful. Just delightful."

"He should get a job with the Tucson Tourist Agency. He pointed out many highlights on our trip from the airport. I'm Douggy—aka Denny Martino." He tips his fedora in my direction.

"Nice to meet the two of you." I turn back toward the group. "Okay, then, I will leave you all to your practice. Thank you again for your participation. Help yourself to the food table in the back. Guests will arrive as early as 6:15, and the show starts at 7:00." I smile, allowing myself a long, deep breath. "The program simply lists your names and stage personas. Per the request of many of you," I say, looking particularly at Sherman and Nancy, who blushes, "I'm leaving you all this chance to figure out the order of your performance. Remember, please, that this is a final send-off concert before many of our residents head back to their homes for the summer. There are going to be many people here who can't wait to celebrate this night with you. You each get three songs. Please cooperate as you set the order of performance." I make eye contact with everyone standing in front of me though I linger a second longer upon Sherman Padowski. "Mario will be available if you need help with prop set-ups." Mario raises his hand as a way of introduction. "And to answer an earlier question, the paychecks will come *after* the performance, ensuring that everyone performs according to the contract." I don't smile because I feel like I'm parenting a group of difficult teenagers that need to be reminded who is the boss. When I am satisfied that everyone has received my warning, I replace the scowl on my face with a smile. "Again, we are so excited to have you all here in Tucson Valley. JJ, your job is most important as you will be introducing each of the acts…"

"In addition to singing my *own* songs, not somebody's *else's* songs," he snorts, judging the group in front of him, as he slicks back his gray hair, making him look younger than his years.

"Yes, in addition to singing your own songs." Play nice is what I want to say, but instead I clap my hands twice and send them to practice, hoping against hope that this show will go off without any more problems. Hope is a fickle thing, of course.

Chapter 7

Tracy and I are eating Chinese takeout in her office when we hear the problem first. Shouting. Lots of shouting. I hold my head in my hands and rub my forehead.

"Do you want me to go?" she asks. She raises an eyebrow in concern more for me than for the problems brewing in the auditorium.

"No. You assigned me this babysitting job. I need to babysit."

Tracy chuckles. "I did tell you that the job would never be boring." She pats the top of my hand. "But seriously, if you need me to play superintendent to your principal, please let me know."

I check my phone. It's 5:30. They have 45 minutes to be off that stage before the doors open for people to take their seats. 45 minutes. I enter the auditorium through a stage door in the back, so no one knows I am there. Elena and Xander stand together on one side of the stage—Sunny and Star. The Sinclairs, Clyde and Sherman, stand in the middle. Douggy and Kenny—Denny Martino and Tommy Davis Jr. stand near them. Nancy—Martha Franklin— stands just offstage as if awaiting her turn. What an odd mix of people representing the 1960s, though I know the audience is going to love them. JJ McMeadows holds court as he stands below the stage yelling a string of obscenities that don't seem to be directed at any one person.

"You're wrong, JJ," says Sherman. Even from a distance I can tell that his face is as red as a tomato. "We can't *both* sing that song. It's called 'My Way,' not 'Our Way!'"

Clyde throws his water bottle onto the floor and stomps across the stage until he is standing next to Elena who is texting on her phone. "I can't take it anymore! I can't work with that man!" It's the most emotion I've seen from Clyde in the last 24 hours. I'm kind of impressed, too, because he'd seemed wimpy to me putting up with Sherman's arrogance. What I guess is the most pressing problem right now, though, is two alpha personalities in JJ and Sherman battling it out for control.

At the moment I am about to insert myself into the conversation—argument, really—Elena clears her throat to speak. "Excuse me, boys. You both sound and look a..m..a..z..i..n..g," she draws out slowly. "That song depresses me. Each of you choose a different song. Skip the duets. Filly Sinclair has an incredible song list from which to choose. Do you think that could work, boys?" She pauses for them to answer, neither of them looking her directly at her face. "For the people, boys. Come on now," she says again. She flashes her charming smile.

They each slowly look up and scan the group of performers before them though I can't see their faces from the back. I gather that Elena's mere appearance has cast a spell of sorts. I wonder if she's done more than cast a spell over any of these men, even though she's decades younger than most of them.

"I want 'That's Life,'" Clyde says shortly.

"And I want 'Strangers in the Night,'" Sherman says, winking at Elena, which I do see as he turns to walk off the stage as if no one can dispute his choice.

"Very well then. It's settled."

"With all these shenanigans, we are down to less than an hour to get ready! Martha needs time! I need time!" Nancy says as she pivots backstage and walks to her dressing room, passing me without any acknowledgment of my presence. I can't for the life of me understand where there is room on her face to add any more makeup.

I step back into the hallway behind the stage before anyone sees me. The problem seems averted. I am in awe at Elena Templeton's power. And I am grateful. When I return to my office, there is a long, thin box sitting on my desk. I pluck off the card underneath the big red bow that surrounds the box. *Proud of you. Break a leg! Keats*

I smile as I open the box. I inhale the sweet yellow roses, feeling all of my stress wash away, if only for a moment in time. It's been a long time since anyone has given me flowers. Of course Keaton would be so thoughtful to send me flowers as if it were me on stage tonight.

"We're ready," Mario says, sticking his head into my office. "Everyone is changing in their dressing rooms now."

"Thank goodness. You've been a lifesaver, Mario."

He smiles. "I just do what I'm told. I like Tracy," Mario whispers as I strain to hear him. "But she should have hired you five years ago. You're a lot better organized."

"Thanks, Mario. But I wouldn't have been available five years ago, so everything in it's right time, I guess."

"I suppose that's true. Hey! Do you mind if I sit with my wife in the audience during the show? We secured some great tickets—a perk of the job," he grins.

"Absolutely! I'll hang out backstage in case anyone needs anything. Then I'm running the lights up in the booth. Enjoy the show with Celia."

At 6:15, I unlock the doors to the auditorium. Mom and Jan collect the tickets at the ticket table. They have also been given prime seats, along with their husbands, for their efforts. Mom's been acting like a teenager meeting her idol. What she sees in JJ McMeadows I'll never understand because to me he's an arrogant, spoiled, entitled prima donna. Perhaps he's hardened with age.

I stand at the bottom of the stage on the auditorium floor. It's a good thing most of these ladies don't have the strength of their youth as I imagine some of them would try jumping on stage when they see JJ. I wonder if any of them have considered throwing their bra. I chuckle to myself, imagining Brenda and Jan competing for JJ's attention.

"Rosi!" Bob Horace calls my name as he holds Karen's hand. His beard is freshly trimmed, and he's wearing a sports coat. Karen is dressed in a simple tan skirt and red top, but her face shines.

"Hi, guys. I'm so glad you could come."

"We wouldn't miss this concert for anything," says Karen.

I recall Karen's sweet story about attending a JJ McMeadows's concert with her husband, and it brings joy to my heart. "I am most looking forward to your participation in the final song!"

"Oh! We are so excited about being chosen to participate in the finale. Wait until you see our outfits, Rosi!"

"Oh no!" I smack myself in the forehead. "I didn't designate a changing room for the three of you!"

"It's okay! Elena and Nancy are so sweet. After Douggy and Kenny sing, we're going to slip into their dressing room and get changed. Our outfits are already there!"

"Awesome. I'm so glad they are accommodating." *Unlike some of the men* I want to add. "Have a wonderful evening!" Bob leads Karen to their seats near the front stage door for easy access. Again, I marvel that his last girlfriend was Salem Mansfield.

"Hi, Rosi," says Frank, Jan's husband, the decent one in that duo. He's walking with a couple I presume to be Allen's parents. Allen's mother scowls as she passes by. I dodged a bullet there. Like mother, like son.

By 6:50, all of the seats are taken except for Mom and Jan who will wait by the ticket table until 7:00. Mario is escorting Celia to her seat. She looks like a lovely woman, slightly plump with bright red hair that shines under the house lights. They are talking with Paula and her husband. It's going to be odd not seeing so many of these people in a few weeks when they leave for the summer to spread out across the country back to their homes. I imagine that my job should settle down at least. And I can finally find a place to live that isn't with my parents.

Tracy dims the lights at exactly 7:00. A hush falls over the auditorium. Our audiovisual husband/wife team of Sandra and Chuck Hinten sit in the front row of the audience, a perk for working part time at the senior center. They both worked in Los Angeles in the film industry in the lighting departments of several big films. I'd had a most lovely conversation with Sandra about her experiences with George Clooney on the set of "Batman and Robin." I'm happy to report that he is as lovely in person as he appears in public. But tonight, I've given Sandra and Chuck the night off to enjoy the music of their youth. I've learned enough in my last two months here to run the spotlight. At 7:01, according to the lineup that JJ McMeadows has provided me with, I shine the light on center stage. Kenny pulls the curtain open from backstage, and JJ McMeadows walks on stage to a thunderous applause and roar from his admiring fans. He wears skintight black jeans with a matching black vest over a gray t-shirt that shows off his biceps, which are still pretty impressive for a man in his 70s. I wish I could see Mom's face as she's seeing her childhood crush for the first time in person.

"Ladies and gentlemen, thank you all for coming to the 1960s Extravaganza at Tucson Valley Retirement Community!"

The audience cheers loudly.

"It is an honor to be chosen as the only live act who actually performed successfully during that decade." The crowd laughs. I roll my eyes. His ego is unhinged. "No, no, I'm only joking. We have quite a treat for you tonight with fantastic impersonators of some of your favorites from the '60s performing some of your beloved songs. Speaking of favorites, though, how about we start off with a little song you might remember called 'Moonlight Under Paradise' by yours truly?"

That's my cue to raise the lights to their highest power as JJ sings his song. I admit that I've heard the song played many times on the oldies station, but I also admit there's nothing about the song that makes me want to add it to my Spotify favorite playlist, even hearing it sung live. However, the audience disagrees, and they are the demographic that love him after all. I wonder if they'd love him as much if they knew his arrogance. Probably so.

Filly Sinclair 1, Sherman, comes out next. He's wearing a gray suit and fedora with shiny black shoes that reflect from the spotlight I'm shining on him. He sings three Sinclair songs, none of which are "My Way." I'm impressed that the performers had the thought to sandwich Sunny and Star in between the Sinclairs so as to cut down on unnecessary comparisons. Elena looks beautiful in her silver, body-hugging gown with her natural black hair lying just above her chest which she isn't afraid to display. The dress shimmers under the spotlight. She's younger than the other performers, a contemporary of mine unlike the others who are in their fifties and sixties, except for Sunny, her duo partner. They drive the crowd crazy with their rendition of "I Got You, Babe" though Elena carries the duo with her singing talent. And when Elena trips on her way off the stage, JJ catches her in his arms so assuredly that a new round of applause breaks out. This night is a bigger hit than I could have imagined.

"And now, ladies and gentlemen, please welcome back to the stage, Filly Sinclair…2," he adds.

I envision Clyde's face falling as he hears this introduction, especially since he was the *first* Sinclair hired. I see Brenda from my vantage point in the audio-visual booth. She leans forward in her seat as if expectantly hoping he will flub up a line or fall on the stage. He tips his imaginary hat at Brenda never knowing that she is the reason for all his stresses this week. George sits still next to her, I imagine, not cracking so much as a smile. She may not have exactly the same reputation as Salem Mansfield did with the men in Tucson Valley, but she's a flirt. And she thinks she's eighteen again with her surgically perky breasts and over-highlighted hair and skintight mini skirt. She likes Clyde's attention. I know it. Clyde sings an equal number of songs as Sherman to the same applause. That should satisfy them both.

Douggy and Kenny duet together, some of Denny Martino and Tommy Davis Jr.'s hits. They look suave and relaxed in their matching black suits. There's something to be admired about performers who take pride in the sophistication of their appearance.

"Hey, cutie," I hear from behind me in the booth.

"Keats, you scared me!"

"Sorry. Thought you might want some company."

I grin. "Was your tenth-row complimentary seat not good enough for you?" I whisper.

"Truthfully, it was kind of lonely."

I hold up my hand to quiet him for a second as I move the strobe light back to JJ McMeadows who is singing his third song of the evening. The audience members act like sixteen-year-olds at a Taylor Swift concert. It's undeniably cute.

"I'm glad you're here," I say to Keaton who has pulled up a folding chair next to me. "But no distractions! This is serious business."

He kisses me on the cheek, and I playfully push him away. "I'm serious!" I whisper as loud as acceptable without disturbing the crowd below though it's impossible they'd hear me.

"No more distractions," Keaton mouths.

After JJ sings, Nancy walks onto the stage dressed as Martha Franklin. Actually, she sashays onto the stage, owning it more and more with every step she takes to the center. When she fluffs up her red boa, the crowd goes wild. Even Dad appears to be hooting and hollering from his seat next to Mom. I'd be embarrassed if it weren't for the fact that everyone else was eating up Nancy's performance, too. Nancy sings two Martha Franklin classics: "Respect" and "A Natural Woman." By the time she sings the last note, the entire audience—at least those who are able—are on their feet and applauding loudly.

"I think you have a happy crowd," Keaton says.

I shake my head in awe at how well this night has gone after all of the demands and stresses and hiccups along the way. From the back of the stage come Karen, Paula, and Brenda dressed in purple miniskirts—with Brenda's being the miniest of all—and white shirts with black feather boas. They each stand behind a microphone stand, the smiles on their faces emanating joy to everyone in the crowd. George sits behind a drum set, a purple bandana tied around his forehead. Bob holds his trumpet proudly, and Leo straps on his guitar, each of them wearing purple bowties. I am loving the color-coordination.

"Welcome Tucson Valley's finest to the stage for our 1960s medley!" JJ points to George who taps the cymbals. *1, 2, 3.* And, to my amazement, every performer upon the stage sings melodies from some famous 1960s classics including "California Dreamin'," "Daydream Believer," and "Runaway" while our residents sing backup and play musical accompaniment. It's perfect. Seriously, it's outstanding. I am shocked.

One final curtain call with all of the performers linking hands and bowing as JJ McMeadows sings "Love Beats, Heartbeats," closes out the show. Tracy pulls the curtain cord, an update the auditorium also needs to make, closing the curtain and the performers behind it. I kill the spotlights. Mario has jumped out of his seat to turn on the auditorium lights. I take a bow before Keaton, reveling in a most successful evening. The crowd dissipates with many stopping to get autographs and pictures with the performers in the hallway, JJ's line being the longest. I spy Mom in Sherman's line and consider asking her to move to Clyde's line instead when I realize he's not amongst the performers in the hallway.

"Thank you, darling," JJ is saying to Karen as he kisses her on the cheek. She beams with adoration as she and Bob walk hand in hand out of the performing arts center. She's still wearing her purple miniskirt.

Elena and Nancy pose together for a picture with Frank as Jan stands by giving them the stink eye.

"Great night, huh?" asks Tracy as she startles me from behind, linking her arm through mine. Keaton has gone to help Mario put away the chairs we'd added to the back row.

"I think it was a memorable night. Everyone seemed to have a fun time."

"They sure did, Rosi. I'm already hearing buzz about repeating the show next year."

"Oh, geez." I hit myself in the forehead. "I don't know if I can do this again in 365 days.

Tracy laughs. "Sure you can. You're a pro now."

I take a moment to admire the people in front of us, chattering with friends, smiling, waiting for pictures, enjoying life. I'm reminded about the value of living in a community where the main goal for living each day is to find the joy.

But my thoughts are interrupted as a commotion from inside the auditorium takes my breath away. A blood-curding scream echoes against the walls and wafts into the hallway, causing everyone to stop talking mid-conversation. "He's dead! He's dead!"

Chapter 8

I follow Tracy who is following the sound of the scream that continues. The sounds lead us to the far side of the stage nearest the emergency exit. Brenda, still dressed in her purple miniskirt, is clutching her head and leaning over something that lies at the base of the stage. George stands up from the ground, blocked at first by Brenda. When they see Tracy and me, they say nothing but point to the ground.

"What happened?" cries Tracy.

"Has anyone called 911?"

Brenda shakes her head back and forth. "Oh, for the love of men!" I pull out my cellphone and punch in the numbers. "I'm not sure. It looks bad. Okay. Yes." I set down the phone, and for the second time since my arrival at Tucson Valley Retirement Community I am checking the pulse of a body that looks very much dead. Only this time I know the person. "There is no pulse," I say as I pick up the phone. "Yes, I understand. We won't touch a thing. Thank you."

I stand up and look from Tracy to Brenda to George to the ten or fifteen people who now surround us. "The police are on their way." I feel my chest tighten, squeeze my eyes shut, and exhale quickly. I don't realize that Keaton stands next to me until he puts an arm around my waist.

Tracy looks at Brenda, scrunching up her face in consideration before she speaks. "What did you do?" she asks quietly.

Brenda gasps. "Me? You think I did this? I didn't do this. I didn't do anything! I only found him! George and me..." She looks at her husband who wrinkles his face as he stares at the man lying before him as if his gaze is magnetically drawn to the body. "Tell them, George."

George only nods his head slowly, not looking at his wife. Then he turns his back on us and vomits all over the auditorium floor.

"What's the commotion?" asks Nancy who is walking toward us from atop the stage, her stage gown replaced with a Juicy Couture hot pink track suit. She's removed her wig and her false lashes. She stops at the point on the stage where she is just above the body that lies splayed upon the ground, fresh blood flowing from his head, a broken bottle of Tucson Valley Honey Wine still dripping down the stage. "Sherman!" she screams, stumbling forward.

For a moment I think we are going to have to catch Nancy as she topples off the stage. Xander and Elena run onto the stage, each reaching for an arm just in time as they spy Sherman Padowski for the first time. Elena's eyes look like mini-Frisbees.

"I think we should back away from the scene," says Tracy. "The police will be here soon. Please, everyone, have a seat at the back of the auditorium until the police can sort this…this tragedy out," says Tracy.

I snap out of my shock and shake my head in agreement. "Yes, please, everyone. Let's have a seat."

"Why on earth would we want to stay a second longer?" Brenda shrieks. "This is…this is disgusting!" she sobs as she steps back from Sherman's body. Everyone else steps back, too, to let her through as she runs out of the auditorium. I put my hand on George's shoulder. "You can't let her leave, George. The police will want to talk to her."

"I know," he says sadly. "I know." He runs his fingers through the strands of hair that remain atop his head. "Sorry about that," he says, pointing to his vomit.

"It's okay. We will clean it up." The crowd of people scatter from the scene, taking Tracy's direction. "George, what happened?"

He bobs his head absently as if in a fog. "I don't know, Rosi. Brenda told me she needed a permanent marker for autographs. When she didn't come back, I went looking for her. Then I heard her scream, just before you all came in here."

I realize that George's hand is shaking. He's in shock. "Have a seat, George. I'll send Keaton to find Brenda."

"Yes, that's a good idea. Come along, George. There's a comfortable seat over here." George follows Keaton to the back of the auditorium where he sits.

"I'll get him some water," says Tracy.

"What's going on, Rosi?"

I turn to see Mario, dressed in his work clothes again, jeans and a t-shirt, standing behind me. "Mario, I am so glad to see you."

"I took Celia home because I know there's some clean up to do, but why are all of these people still here?"

I step aside so that he can see the body. He throws his hand over his open mouth. "What happened to Sherman?"

"It looks like someone hit him with a bottle of wine, and he fell—or was pushed—off the stage."

"Is he…?"

"Yes. He is most definitely dead. But the vomit is from George. He and Brenda found the body."

"Oh my…"

"Rosi?" I recognize that voice. I look up to see Officer Dan Daniel with his new partner Officer Emma Prince. She'd been introduced to me her first week on the job when Officer Daniel stopped by for a visit. We've become a version of friends ever since working together on Salem Mansfield's case. It's more of a *how ya been* kind of friendship, but I trust him a heck of a lot more than I did when I first arrived in Tucson Valley.

"I'm glad you're here." I mean it, too. I wave at Officer Prince.

"Fill me in?"

"To start, the show was fantastic. The performers received a standing ovation. After a few moments, some of them met fans and signed autographs in the hallway. Then we heard a scream. It was Brenda…"

"Brenda ….?"

"Yes. Brenda Riker and her husband George found the body. George got sick to his stomach." I indicate the pile of vomit. "I checked for a pulse. Otherwise, nothing has been touched to my knowledge."

"Are George and Brenda still here?"

I point to George who is now sitting with my dad. I had completely forgotten that my parents were likely still in the building. "Keaton went after Brenda. She was pretty upset." I don't like the woman one bit, but I understand quite well how disturbing it is to fall upon a dead body.

Officer Daniel shakes his head up and down several times and rubs his chin. "I'd like for you to ask all of the people still in the building to leave their names and numbers with Officer Prince. We need to get their statements, find out if anyone saw anything. Do you know if anyone saw anything, Rosi?"

I shake my head back and forth. "No. I have no idea what happened, just what I've told you."

"And who is the victim? I suppose I should have led with that question."

Out of the corner of my eye I see Keaton leading Brenda back into the auditorium and pointing toward George and my dad. "His name is Sherman Padowski. He's a Filly Sinclair impersonator. He was one of our star performers this evening."

"Huh. Interesting. Someone had a grudge against Filly Sinclair."

"I don't think anyone had a grudge against Filly Sinclair. But I can attest to the fact that preparations for tonight's show haven't exactly been smooth."

"Can you elaborate?"

"I can but not here." I lean close to Officer Daniel so that he is the only one that can hear me. "There were a lot of egos on display today—and tonight."

The last thing I want to do is accuse anyone of a crime unfairly. I'd seen the effect it had had on Bob Horace when he'd been arrested for Salem's murder, and I refuse to do that to another person. But it's clear that Sherman did not fall off that stage. Someone smashed his head with a bottle of wine.

"It can't wait until tomorrow, Rosi. There might be a murderer loose in the building as we speak."

I shudder involuntarily. That thought had not occurred to me. I look out over the scatterings of people that sit in the auditorium seats, probably twenty-five people or so left including Mom, Dad, George and Brenda, Jan and Frank, Paula and her husband, Mayor Leo, and a lot of people I've seen but never met. Officer Prince is moving amongst the crowd writing information down on a clipboard. Keaton and Mario stand at the base of the left side of the stage. "I'm going to check on the performers in their dressing rooms."

"Good idea. And please tell them not to go anywhere. How many performers were here tonight?"

"Seven, well, eight, if you include JJ McMeadows, the emcee."

"That guy with the 'Dance Craze' song?"

"Yep, that's the one."

"My mom loves that guy."

"Too bad she couldn't come tonight."

Officer Daniel points to Sherman Padowski who has now been covered with a sheet by the crime investigation team, if you can call a single person a team. "Perhaps it's good that she wasn't available tonight."

"Yeah, fair point."

Tracy intercepts me on my way to the dressing rooms. "Rosi, what are we going to do? This is just terrible. Our reputation is on the line!" She talks so quickly I think she is going to hyperventilate.

"Tracy, we didn't do anything wrong. The senior center didn't do anything wrong. Something tragic happened here, but it's going to be okay." I place a hand on each shoulder and look her square in the eyes when I say the next thing. "But the real problem will be if Officer Daniel can't solve this mystery quickly because there could be a very bad man—or woman—in this building."

"Like, right now?" she asks.

"Yes," I whisper.

"I don't like this, Rosi."

"I don't, either. Can you do me a favor?"

She nods her head. "I need you to find Sherman's contract in my office. There's a file folder on my desk marked *contracts*." I think her eyes light up when I say *file folder*. Printed contracts in file folders rather than stuck in emails on a computer are still something I can support. "Officer Daniel is going to have to contact Sherman's family. I need to check on the performers in their dressing rooms."

"And it was such a great night," Tracy mutters over and over to herself as she walks toward my office.

It really was.

The first door I knock on belongs to Elena and Nancy. "Excuse me? It's Rosi. May I come in?" I ask softly.

"Come in." Nancy's gregarious voice rings out clearly, even in a time like this. "Sit down, sweetie," she says, pointing to a folding chair across from her. She's sitting in an old recliner someone had donated to the senior center when they'd updated their furniture. The flowers on the arms of the chair have faded to dull greens and blues becoming threadbare.

Elena sits across from Nancy on a gold-colored chaise. She's changed into a pair of black yoga pants and a pink crop top, her long, black hair pulled into a high ponytail. Her makeup has smeared down her face in long, zebra stripes as if the effort itself to wipe away the tears was too painful.

I sit down across from Nancy with Elena at my side. "I wanted to check in on the two of you, to see if you need anything."

"Do we need to change our travel plans, Rosi? I'm supposed to catch a plane back to Vegas tomorrow morning real early," says Nancy.

She takes a long drink from a glass of wine, the wine from the gift basket I'd given to all of the entertainers. It strikes me for the first time that I'd possibly purchased the murder weapon used to smash Sherman Padowski over the head.

"Rosi?" asks Elena softly.

"S...sorry. I was thinking that perhaps that question is best for Officer Daniel or Officer Prince. They've asked that everyone in the building remain until they've gotten contact information."

Nancy's eyes grow large. "You don't suppose that a murderer is still in the building, do you?"

"I really don't know."

"Does that door lock?" Nancy asks, pointing to the door of the pathetic excuse for a dressing room.

I walk over to the door to try the lock. It does not work. "Sorry. We've never had to worry about anything like this before."

"Help me move this chair before you go," says Nancy as she jumps up from the recliner and gets into position to shove it across the room to block the door. Elena doesn't move from her perch on the chaise lounge.

"Do you really think that's necessary? The police are in the building now. Everyone is fully aware of what is happening around them," I say, wondering if this day will ever end.

"I'm not taking any chances," says Nancy. "I've got a big week of performances, not to mention a lifetime of fun," she says, running her hands over her ample curves. "I'm not letting any nutball get in my way."

I catch Elena rolling her eyes, but Nancy doesn't see her. I help Nancy move the cumbersome chair closer to the door, leaving room for me to scoot out before the final push. "Please make sure to let the officers in when they get backstage. Perhaps you'll be able to leave then. Oh! And I'll be back with your paychecks. I almost forgot. Sorry."

"It's okay, Rosi." Nancy pats me on the head. "It's been a hard night for *all* of us. But especially for poor Sherman," she whispers. At the mention of Sherman's name, Elena makes an audible sob that startles us both. "I think she's extra sensitive," she whispers as she closes the door behind me. I hear the chair pushed against the door and wonder if I should be more afraid than I am.

Chapter 9

I decide to return to my office for the paychecks, so I don't have to make a second visit to all of the performers tonight. I really want to be done with them once the police have gathered the information they need. I need this building to be empty so I can clear my mind and figure out how to clean up this mess, literally and figuratively.

I use the key in my pocket to open the safe behind my desk. I pull out the checks, each organized into an individual envelope with the person's name. Sherman Padowski's envelope is on top. I think about my interactions with Sherman over the last thirty-six hours. He'd clearly irritated Clyde and tangled with JJ for alpha control of the room, but he hadn't done anything to warrant losing his life, though is there ever a good justification for murder?

"There you are, Rosi!"

I jump in surprise when I hear my name.

"Sorry! I didn't mean to scare you. But Officer Daniel is looking for you. He sent me to find you."

"Okay, Jan. Thanks. I'll be right there." She doesn't leave. I feel her watching me as I close the safe.

"This turned into a crap show, didn't it?" I imagine the smug look on her face before I turn around for confirmation.

"A great evening has ended in tragedy," I say solemnly.

"Hmph. That's the understatement of the night. Don't you find it odd, Rosi, that Tucson Valley has been a quiet community for years, and since you've come to town there have now been not one but *two* murders you have been involved in?" She puts one hand on the hip that is not leaning against the doorframe of my office.

I squint my eyes at this woman that despises me because I rebuffed her nephew as if I've committed a mortal sin. "Are you implying that I had something to do with Sherman's murder because if you are, you've crossed a line, Jan." I can feel the heat radiating from my red face.

"Of course not—although—well…"

"Well what, Jan?" I shut off my office light, so she has to back out of the room.

"Darkness can follow people. And perhaps you've brought darkness to Tucson Valley."

I've never wanted to slap someone in my life, even Wes after I found out he'd been sleeping with Cara in our bed. But I want to slap Jan Jinkins. I want to slap her and push her to the ground. I want to…Oh my go…is this how Sherman was murdered? Someone got so angry with him that they turned to violence. I clench and unclench my fists, get as close to her face as possible, and spit out my words instead of my fists. "Go to hell, Jan." Then I push past, leaving her shocked in my wake.

Officer Daniel is about to go into Clyde, Douggy, and Xander's dressing room when he sees me. "Hey, Rosi. Glad Jan found you."

"She found me alright!" I hiss.

"Is there a problem?"

"No, sorry. What did you need?"

"Officer Prince has gotten all the contact information we need from the people in the auditorium. We've told them to go home. The coroner is coming for the body, and I'm bringing in someone to clean up the scene. Once I've cleared out the performers, I need to sit down and go over a few things with you, but I realize it's late. Can we just have a short chat tonight and then a longer one tomorrow morning?"

I focus on his large nose as I try to steady my breathing. "Yeah, sure," I shake my head. "Of course. Thanks, Dan."

"Rosi." He says my name so softly it catches me off guard. "You didn't do anything wrong."

"How do you…how…?"

"Because this was your show. In the last hour, I have heard countless reviews about what a fantastic night it's been. That's because of you and your hard work. Don't hold yourself responsible for what happened *after* the show."

"Thanks, Dan." I think back to my early interactions with Officer Daniel that hadn't been most positive. "Do you mind if I come in there with you?" I ask, pointing to the names of Filly Sinclair, Denny Martino, and Sunny Moon on the placards I'd made the previous day. "I need to pay them."

"Sure. It will be like the old days," he says, winking at me.

Douggy and Xander are scrolling through their phones. Clyde is lying on an old beanbag chair I'd found when we were clearing out the storage under the stage. They focus on Officer Daniel the minute they see him.

"Officer, what's going on?" asks Douggy. "When can we go?"

"Soon. But I need to get some information first. I'm Officer Daniel. You know Rosi," he points to me. They all shake their heads in agreement. "I need to get your names and contact information. I also have a few questions for each of you."

"Of course. We'll do anything you need," Clyde says a little too eagerly. He's still wearing his Filly Sinclair suit, though it's quite wrinkled from lying in the beanbag chair. The others have changed—Douggy into jeans and Xander into running pants.

"Good. Let's start with the big question. What were you doing immediately after the show tonight? I'll start with you," he says, pointing to Douggy.

"Sure. I'm Douggy Carson. I play Denny Martino in the show." He tips an imaginary hat at Officer Daniel who does not smile. "After our final song, I came backstage to grab a bottle of water from the awesome spread Rosi set out for us. I was parched. What a night! I mean, there were so many smiling faces in that crowd. It was electric!" he says as if reliving the glorious moment. "Then I went to the john and came out into the hallway to meet my fans and sign autographs."

"And did you see Mr. Padowski after the show?"

"I did. He was waiting in line for the toilet when I came out. He told me *good show* kind of like you'd tell your opponents *good game* after a basketball game which I thought was pretty funny. Otherwise, I didn't see him again until all that screaming and commotion from the auditorium."

"And you went to the john within how many minutes of everyone stepping off the stage?"

"Probably five minutes. I really had to go, man! You know how it is. But even though I made a beeline for the john, I wasn't the first person there." He laughs and makes a face as if repulsed. "There was a pretty nasty stink in that bathroom!"

No one responds to his comment. "And Mr. ....?" Officer Daniel asks, pivoting to Clyde who has sat down on a folding chair that looks like it could topple over at any minute. I make a mental note to throw it out.

"Clyde Andrews. I'm a Filly Sinclair impersonator," he says sadly.

Officer Daniel looks confused, touching the tip of his long nose as if trying to smell out the reason for his confusion. "I thought that Mr. Padowski was the Sinclair act."

Clyde sighs. "There were two of us," he says. "I was asked first, but Sherman had a connection to Tucson Valley and was brought in as a second impersonator, though he thought of himself as the number one Sinclair." Clyde tries to smooth out the wrinkles of his suit jacket to no avail.

"Uh-huh. What's the connection, Rosi?" he turns to me for confirmation.

I sigh. This isn't going to look good for Clyde. "Sherman Padowski is Brenda Riker's cousin's wife's brother."

"Cousin's wife's brother," Officer Daniel repeats slowly, trying to work it out in his head. "And I presume that Brenda made an, uh, request that Sherman participate in this show?"

"You nailed it," I say.

"He wasn't even supposed to be here," Clyde says irritated. "If only that woman had kept her nose out of this business, Sherman would still be alive."

"And where were you after the show?"

Douggy, Xander, Officer Daniel, and I look expectantly at Clyde, as if we are all willing him to have a good answer because it's hard to hide his distaste for the victim.

"I stepped outside for a smoke," he says quietly. "I'm a stress smoker. My wife would have a fit if she knew I was smoking."

I'm reminded of Mom's nasty habit that she hides from Dad. "Out front?" I ask.

"No. There's an exit door from the auditorium that is just past the front row of seats."

Officer Daniel looks at me, and I nod my head in agreement. "It's the door next to where Sherman's body was found at the base of the stage." I catch a look of realization that crosses Clyde's face.

"Did you see Mr. Padowski when you came in from your smoke?" asks Officer Daniel.

"I sure as heck did. I saw him about the same time everyone else did when Brenda started screaming like a madwoman. If you ask me, that's where you should be looking. She's been nothing but trouble this week."

He's not wrong. Brenda's interfering only ratcheted up the emotions between Sherman and Clyde, but I highly doubt she could commit murder, and why on earth would she kill the man she championed all week? If it had been Clyde on the ground on the other hand... I let my mind wander with possibilities and *what-ifs*.

"Was there anyone else smoking with you outside, Mr. Andrews?"

"Of course not. You think I'd like to make this nasty habit any more acceptable by sharing it with a smoking buddy? Look, I'm sorry. I'm really, really sorry. It's been a long day. I can't believe any of this is happening."

Xander, still wearing his Sunny Moon wig, stands up and pats Clyde on the shoulder in a kind of *it's going to be okay, buddy* gesture. "Officer Daniel, I'm Xander Nolan. I was Sunny Moon in the show tonight." Even as a short man, Officer Daniel looks down at Xander. He takes off his wig and holds his hand out which Officer Daniel takes in greeting. I notice that Xander's hair is the same black color of his wig and wonder why he didn't just grow his hair out naturally to look like Sunny Moon.

"Nice to meet you, Mr. Nolan. Might you tell me where you were right after the show?"

"Sure. I came back to my dressing room for a drink, put on some fresh deodorant because that spotlight was hot," he says, arching an eyebrow at me as if I could control the temperature from the spotlight. "And then I went to greet my fans."

"Did you have any conversations with anyone on your way to the hallway to greet your, uh, fans," he says sarcastically. I try not to laugh.

"I did. I talked with Star, my singing partner," he says. "Elena."

"In your dressing room or hers?" I ask. Officer Daniel looks at me as if to remind me that he is the professional—not me—but I can't help myself. All of those newspaper story sleuthing skills are dying to be used, perhaps a bad word choice.

"Neither. I talked to Elena as we grabbed a bite to eat on our way to our dressing rooms."

"But you said you had a drink in your dressing room."

"I did," Xander says, clearly annoyed that Officer Daniel doesn't seem to be following his story. "We grabbed a little food from the food table Rosi had set up for us, and I poured a glass of wine in my dressing room before preparing to meet with the audience and sign autographs."

"And did you?"

"Sign autographs?" Xander asks. "Of course I did! I even brought headshots that I signed for free. It was a blast!" His eyes shine as if he were on top of the world. "Man, were they eating up our show tonight. That crowd was rocking!"

"Did any of you see Sherman after the show—except at the toilet?" I ask the obvious question that hasn't yet been asked.

Clyde, Xander, and Douggy look at each other, and all shake their head no. A knock on the door welcomes another performer into the room. "Hey!" says Kenny. He seems surprised to see us all in the room. He's wearing a plain white t-shirt and boxers, as if he's preparing for bed. I consider stepping outside of the room, but he doesn't seem bothered by my presence.

"Hello," says Officer Daniel. "Might you also be a performer from tonight's show?"

"Yeah, I'm Tommy Davis Jr.—Kenny."

"Mr.—"

"Davis," he says.

"I mean, what is your real last name, not your stage last name."

"Davis," he repeats. "Both last names are Davis. Pretty cool, huh?" He smiles for the first time since entering the room.

"Mr. Davis, I'd like to know what you were doing after the show tonight."

"Sure, Sherman and I drank manuka honey green tea in our dressing room."

"Manuka honey?" he asks.

"Yeah, JJ says it's supposed to be soothing for your throat after a big show—some kind of natural anti-inflammatory properties. Seemed kind of wacko to Sherman and me, but we didn't have the heart to tell JJ no when he offered us the tea."

"So, Mr. McMeadows was also in your dressing room?" he asks.

"Just for the amount of time it took to drink the tea."

"We didn't get offered any tea," says Douggy.

"Yeah, that would have been kind of nice," says Xander.

Clyde shakes his head in agreement.

"And what did Mr. Padowski do after you drank tea together?" asks Officer Daniel.

Kenny shrugs his shoulders. "I have no idea. I took a shower," he says.

"A shower?" I ask. "We don't have shower facilities in the performing arts center."

"I know that, but your sports complex is next door. I showered there. It's a 24-hour facility. I read the sign."

Officer Daniel looks at me, and once again, I nod my head in agreement. "Very well, gentleman. Thanks for your time. You are free to go as soon as Officer Prince has gotten your contact information. She will be here soon."

"Thank the Lord," says Douggy. "I've got a gig in New Mexico this week."

"Lucky you," says Kenny. "I don't have anything lined up until the middle of summer."

"Maybe I can put a good word in for you, buddy."

Kenny slaps Douggy on the back. "Thanks. Much appreciated."

I almost forget about the envelopes I am holding. "Wait! Here is your payment." I hand each of the envelopes to its rightful owner. "We really appreciate everything you've done this weekend. I am so sorry that your wonderful show has been tainted by this horrible tragedy.

We'd love to talk about bringing you back to build upon the *positive* parts of Tucson Valley."

"Thanks, Rosi," says Xander. "Everything went perfectly. Don't blame yourself."

"Yeah, it was a fantastic weekend," says Douggy.

Kenny nods in agreement. "We'll be back. All you have to do is ask."

"Thanks. Safe travels home."

Officer Daniel follows me out of their dressing room.

"How much longer will you be here?"

"I need to talk to the female entertainers and the emcee. That will be all for tonight. Do you think I could pick your brain tomorrow morning? We can meet at a coffee shop if you don't want to come to the station. I need to figure out this timeline and sort out everyone's stories."

"Absolutely. I don't think that Tracy and I will be able to focus on anything else but this night for quite some time. Thankfully, our next show in the performing arts center isn't scheduled for three weeks. That is, if they will still come now that there's been a murder on the stage." I shake my head in disbelief.

"What's your next act?"

"An Agatha Christie play featuring seniors from a neighboring retirement community."

"Oof!"

"Yeah. We might need to make some changes. Hey! Can you give these envelopes to Nancy and Elena, please? I'm going to check on the auditorium, make sure everyone has left."

"Sure thing, Rosi. Thanks, as always, for your help."

"I'd really like to stop making this a thing we do together."

He laughs. "But then I might be out of a job."

"Perhaps we could focus on petty theft?"

"Petty theft sounds delightful."

Chapter 10

I stop by JJ McMeadows's dressing room to pay him, but the lights are off. I find Tracy sitting at the back of the auditorium. She's rubbing her forehead like she's trying to work out a headache. I feel her pain. I sit next to her. Neither of us speaks for a moment. We don't need to. We think the same thoughts. How did something like murder happen in our building after one of our most highly anticipated events to one of our performers?

We watch Mario drag a bucket of soapy water in front of the first row of seats. The body has been removed, but Mario will scrub the floor clean. Tomorrow no one will be able to tell that a horrible tragedy happened here tonight—yet everyone will remember. Who could forget? Many in the community were still here, in the same building, when the body was discovered. And worse than having someone die under your watch is to know someone was *killed* under your watch—someone that may have been still in the performing arts centers while Brenda wailed.

"I need to find JJ," I say quietly as we watch Mario work.

"JJ left a long time ago," Tracy says softly.

"I haven't paid him yet."

Tracy shrugs her shoulders. "Send it in the mail."

"That's weird."

"What's weird, Rosi?"

"Officer Daniel hadn't talked to JJ yet."

"Maybe the female officer talked to him."

"Maybe."

"What do you think happened, Rosi?"

"Someone hit Sherman over the head with a wine bottle *that I bought* and shoved him off the stage."

"I don't mean what literally happened. I mean— why do you think it happened? The night radiated energy and excitement. Murders don't happen after nights like that." Tracy shakes her head back and forth in frustration. I have no answer for her.

Keaton surprises us both when he walks into the auditorium with two cups of coffee in to-go cups. "There you are!" He hands a coffee to Tracy and one to me.

"I hope these are decaf," says Tracy. "I need to sleep this night away."

"They are," says Keaton, dropping into the theater seat next to mine.

"Why are you still here? You need to work tomorrow."

"Tomorrow is Sunday, silly. Plus, I thought you might need a cheerful, handsome face to get your mind off…things." He smiles dopily with his tongue hanging out of the side of his mouth like Barley does when she gets really excited.

"Thanks." I don't even have the energy to make a joke. When Keaton sees Mario at the front of the auditorium, he jumps up from his seat to see if he needs help.

"He's a keeper, Rosi. My husband is in bed fast asleep by now oblivious to this whole night. He texted me when he got home from the road at 7:00 and said he was going straight to bed."

"Truck driving is a tough business."

"So is running a premier retirement center," she says, standing up. "Go home, Rosi. I'll lock up when the police are done. We will regroup tomorrow."

"Thanks, Tracy. We'll get through this. I promise." I give her a hug before waving over Keaton and shouting my gratitude to Mario. All I want to do is sleep.

Keaton walks me to my car. Another thought crosses my mind. What if the murderer is watching? What if he or she is still nearby? And then, why is this happening?

"Thanks," I say as I accept his hug. I shiver though it's still in the 70s at even 11:00 at night.

"Do you want me to follow you back to your parents' house?"

"No. I'll be fine. I'm sure they are still awake, wanting to pick my brain dry of every detail I've learned tonight."

"And what have you learned? Did Officer Daniel give you any idea about what he's thinking?"

"No. I was present when he got alibis from all of the men except for JJ McMeadows who apparently left without talking to police."

"He may not have talked to police, but he definitely had a lot to say before he left."

"What do you mean?"

"Mario and I felt kind of helpless with all the commotion going on, so I helped him finish putting the added chairs away behind the stage. Anyway, Mario had gone for another set of chairs, and I was wrangling with a stack that was about to tumble over when I heard shouting coming from one of the dressing rooms."

"Who was shouting?"

"It was definitely JJ. Coming from his dressing room, I could hear him yelling, saying something about *getting him under control and not being a pansy*."

"Do you know who he was talking to?" I never knew I could be so invested in a group of strangers than I am right now by the people I've met in the last two days.

Keaton shakes his head *no*. "Just as I was walking closer to the door to—well, eavesdrop—my not-so-carefully-stacked pile of chairs came tumbling down. I didn't hear anything else from that room, and I had a mess to clean up, too, because one of the chairs hit your food table, and all the water bottles went rolling across the floor. Sorry about that."

"Hmm, that's interesting. Did you see anyone else while you were backstage?"

"Just Brenda and George when he came to get his drum set. She was hollering at him about being embarrassing and why couldn't he be more like Sherman. Then she started crying—not like tears-falling-gently-down-her-face crying but crying like her life depended on it—very vocal. If you ask me, it's Brenda who is the embarrassing one in that relationship. When he saw me, he paused. I swear he was begging me for help—through his eyes. It was bizarre, Rosi. I didn't know what to say, so I just picked up the water bottles."

"I don't know what to think."

"Try to get some sleep. I'm sure Officer Daniel will figure it out," he chuckles.

I raise my eyebrows in a mocking tone. "Let's hope this investigation goes a bit smoother than the last one."

After one final hug, I get into my new car, my first grown-up purchase I'd made since moving to Tucson. I can't use my parents' car forever. Now that I am staying and they are returning to Illinois, I'd decided to sell my car in Illinois and buy something with better fuel mileage. Of course, I still have to return to Illinois to clean out my belongings in my house when it's sold. I'll sell my old car when I'm back, too. It's too much to think about now, though. All I want to do is shut down for a few hours. I *need* to shut down for a few hours.

Chapter 11

Barley won't leave my side this morning as I eat breakfast outside, trying to find the shade even at this time of the day. She jumps onto my lap. For the hundredth time, I wonder how I am going to survive the Arizona heat in the middle of the summer. It's only April, and I'm sweating at 8:00 a.m. "I know, girl. It's going to be your first summer in Arizona, too." I scratch behind her ears and marvel at how much heavier she feels than she did a few weeks ago. She's a deep caramel color that leaves no doubt she is a Golden Retriever. We have playdates with her mother Suzi when Bob and Karen take Suzi for a walk. We visit in the backyard while the dogs frolic and play until they collapse in a heap into their dog beds under the shade of the patio. Mom had insisted on buying Suzi a dog bed, too. Mom and Dad are really going to miss Barley when they return home. At least they'll have their littlest grandkids nearby as my sensible brother waited until he was married, financially stable, and *mature* before he had kids unlike Wes and I who got pregnant after only dating for a couple of months at age 19. I think we did pretty good to stay married for as long as we did.

"Need a refill of your orange juice?" asks Mom who brings a pitcher of fresh-squeezed orange juice to the patio table.

"Sure. That sounds great. I'm meeting Officer Daniel for coffee soon, though, so not too much."

"Helping him solve another murder." She says it like a statement, not a question.

"I'm only telling him what I know about the performers and the show."

"Uh-huh."

"What's that supposed to mean?" I take a long drink of the sweet orange juice. Barley licks the side of my Golden Girls' glass.

"Officer Daniel doesn't know how to solve a case of toilet papering a bunch of cacti in the neighborhood. He can't solve a *second* murder case in a matter of months without help. He trusts you."

"He has Officer Prince now. I don't know her, but I'm sure they can figure it out. Thanks for the orange juice. I'm going to pass off this lap dog to you and get ready. Thanks, Mom." I place Barley onto her lap and kiss Mom on the cheek.

I choose a pair of khaki shorts and a Tucson Valley t-shirt. It's going to be a physical workday as I will help Mario put the performance center back together. I stick my hair into a barrette at the back of my head to keep my hair out of my face, grateful that I received Grandma's Kate's hair color genes and not Grandma Thelma's who fully grayed by the age of forty.

Officer Daniel, dressed in his uniform, his hat sitting on the table, stands up to greet me when I walk to his table in the coffee shop at the back of the Mabel Brown Sports Complex. It's a sweet gesture. "Hi, Dan."

"Thanks for coming, Rosi." He signals the waiter for another cup of coffee.

I guess he's been here a while. I order a chilled coffee.

"I didn't sleep more than a couple of hours last night. I've been going over my notes." He waves his hand over the pile of papers that sit in front of him. "Someone must be lying. The likelihood of someone outside of the center sneaking in to kill Mr. Padowski doesn't make sense. And if it doesn't make sense, then I'm not buying it."

I want to remind him about how he'd jumped on the guilt of Bob Horace pretty hastily without much evidence in his last murder investigation, but I don't mention it. It seems as if Officer Dan Daniel is evolving in his approach to murder cases—all two that he's worked in Tucson Valley. "What can I do to offer assistance?"

"You are the common thread between all of the witnesses—well, at least the witnesses that were with Mr. Padowski just prior to being hit over the head with a bottle and pushed off the stage."

"I guess I am."

"Let's start with the bottle."

"What would you like to know?"

"You mentioned that you'd given everyone a gift basket that included the bottle of wine?"

"I did. I made them each a gift basket."

"Is that normal?"

"Normal?"

"Do you give all of your performers gift baskets?"

"Of course not," I shake my head. "There was nothing normal about this show. Too many prima donnas. I felt pressured to create more dressing rooms and to make them look homey."

"Homey?"

"JJ McMeadows insisted on a private dressing room next to Elena, the Star impersonator. I only have two dedicated dressing rooms backstage. There were eight performers. I gave JJ his own room, and Mario and I cleaned out a couple of storage rooms to make four dressing rooms. The other performers were divided up. I'm telling you, Dan. It's been a crazy few days."

"Why did Mr. McMeadows want a room next to Ms…" he looks at his notes, "Ms. Templeton?"

"I have no idea."

"Did you see them interact this weekend?"

"Not really. She talked a lot with Nancy—Martha, the only other female on the stage. And Xander, of course, because he played Sunny Moon." I really want to tell Officer Daniel about the problems Clyde and Sherman had caused this week with their arguing, but I don't want to throw shade Clyde's way unnecessarily. Sherman was a jerk. It doesn't mean he deserved to be killed, but he pushed buttons, mine included.

"Did you buy bottles only for the performers?" He taps his pen on the table in a series of staccato notes that makes me want to start humming along. I stop before breaking out into song.

"I bought ten bottles—eight for the performers and two to keep in our staffroom." I raise my shoulders, "You never know when you might need to celebrate or be encouraged to finish your day." I laugh uneasily. "I never imagined something like this would happen."

"Back to the bottles. When I was in the dressing room with you last night, I noticed an open bottle of wine. I presume there should be *three* bottles of wine in that room as it was being used by Mr. Andrews, Mr. Carson, and Mr. Nolan?"

"That's right. Do you want me to check when I'm at work? I was going to break down the rooms and tidy things up."

"Wait on that, please. Can we go over things together? Maybe we should have met there instead. I just really like the coffee here." He smiles as the waiter pours him a third cup.

We both look up as Brenda and Jan sit down two tables away from ours. Neither woman makes eye contact with us. "That is a woman I need to speak to again," he says quietly.

"Do you doubt her story from last night?"

"I'm not sure that I doubt her, but she was awfully upset for someone that claims to not know Mr. Padowski very well."

"She's a drama queen and an attention hog."

"I guess. Mind if we head to the center after I take care of this bill? I need to run by the station first."

"Sounds good. I'll leave the tip. Thanks, Dan."

I steel myself for what I am about to do because talking to Brenda Riker and Jan Jinkins is never pleasant, but I also gleefully can't help myself. "Jan, Brenda, hello. Nice to see you lovely ladies this morning." I'm better at lying the older I get. "I hope that Allen's parents enjoyed the show," I say, reminding Jan of the favor I'd done for that wretched man's family.

Jan arches her eyebrows, and I wonder if she's seeing the same plastic surgeon as Brenda. "They did. Thankfully they left before...you know."

"Yes, that was not the encore we were expecting," I acknowledge. "And how are you feeling this morning, Brenda? You looked pretty torn up last night."

"Of course I looked *torn up,* Rosi! I'd just discovered a dead body, and Sherman was a friend, a very good man!" She takes a drink of her coffee, and I spy a small bottle of rum behind the sugar shaker.

"Oh, I'm sorry. I didn't know that you and Sherman were friends. I thought he was only a relative of a relative."

Jan coughs to clear her throat.

"Of course, yes, that's right. He was my cousin's wife's brother."

"Uh-huh." Something is not squaring in this conversation. "Enjoy your coffee," I say, pointing to the bottle of rum. Jan and Brenda exchange looks, perhaps deer caught in headlights?

"Good day, Rosi," says Jan.

I leave to meet Officer Daniel at the performing arts center. I imagine I'm the topic of Jan and Brenda's conversation before I even make it to the parking lot.

Chapter 12

My first stop when I return to work is Tracy's office. She's on the phone and waving me into the seat across from her desk. A pile of file folders scatter across her desk along with at least ten pens even though an empty pen container sits on the edge of the desk next to a picture of her family that looks like it was taken a decade ago.

"Hey, Rosi. Sorry about that. Sherman's assistant called, said she'd left a message on your office phone and couldn't reach you."

"Oh, yeah. I haven't made it down to my office yet. Did you say Sherman's assistant? I didn't know he had an assistant. What's her name?"

"Dee."

"Dee?"

"Yeah, that's her name."

"Huh, weird. JJ had a former assistant named Dee."

Tracy throws up her hands as if she doesn't understand, either. "She wants you to send Sherman's payment."

"For real? Her...uh...*boss* just died, and she's most concerned about his paycheck? That doesn't sit well with me. I think I need to talk to his family and find out where they'd like the check sent, not someone who claims to be his assistant."

"Fine with me. Do you have that information?"

"I have his information from his contract. I'll get further instructions from Officer Daniel when he comes over to walk through the auditorium and backstage again."

"Looking for clues?"

"Yep."

"Rosi, the night rocked. The audience enjoyed themselves immensely. I can't stress enough how many positive messages I've received since last night."

I sigh. "That's great. But from now on, last night—and possibly every event going forward that is held at the Tucson Valley Retirement Community Performing Arts Center—will carry a shadow of darkness with it."

"Not if the murder is solved quickly. Attach a name to the crime, send the person to jail, and I think the community will be able to move on. Have a murderer on the loose—well, that's a problem."

I shake my head in agreement. "Hey! Why are you here this morning?" I ask, realizing that Sunday is a day neither of us come into the office.

"I knew there'd be many calls to field. The HOA board, in particular, has lots of questions about what happened last night."

I laugh. "I can only imagine that they have plenty of opinions. I ran into Jan and Brenda this morning."

"Jan was the first message I returned. She wanted to know if we'd brought in a professional cleaning crew because the thought of returning to the scene of the crime, so to speak, was so repulsive to her that she wanted to make sure no evidence of a crime existed."

"Did she think we'd just leave blood splattered all over the floor in front of the first row of seats?"

"I don't know what some of these people think." She rolls her eyes, which, by the looks of them, tell me that she didn't get much sleep last night either.

"I'll let you know if Officer Daniel comes up with any theories. Feel free to forward any messages you want me to return. I plan on being here most of the day." I stand up to leave.

"Wait! Rosi, do you think that someone local killed Sherman Padowski? Someone from Tucson Valley?"

"I have no idea. It could have been someone local. It could have been another performer. It could have been someone coming through an exit door on the side of the stage for all we know."

"Well, that's not possible."

"Why?"

"Because all of the exit doors are locked. No one can just walk in."

"Are you telling me that if someone were to take a smoke break outside that they would not be able to re-enter?"

"Yes, that's correct. The exit doors adjoining the auditorium lock automatically. Why?"

"No worries. I'll be in touch." I wave goodbye and think about Clyde all the way down to the auditorium. Why would he lie about smoking outside the auditorium?

Officer Daniel is walking down the center aisle toward the stage as I'm entering the auditorium. "Good timing." I say, smiling. "Anywhere in particular you'd like to start?"

Officer Daniel returns my smile. He's not an attractive man by any stretch of the imagination. His nose is too big. He stands an inch shorter than me, and he badly needs a haircut, but now that we're on the same team he's much more enjoyable to work with. "Dressing rooms. Let's start with Mr. McMeadows's room."

"Have you talked with him yet?"

"Nope. I'm still waiting for a call back. I'm getting irritated the longer he takes to call."

"I'm sure he's a very busy man," I raise my eyes in a mocking gesture.

Officer Daniel snorts so loud it sounds like a litter of baby pigs have entered the room. "As busy as a 1960s has-been pop star can be."

"Hey, there were a lot of people here last night who would argue the *has-been* assessment."

I turn the lights on in JJ's dressing room. The placard I'd made for his room is thrown on the coffee table in the middle of the room. "His gift basket is gone, including the wine bottle."

Officer Daniel assesses the room as if trying to take a snapshot with his mind. "That doesn't mean he used the wine bottle to kill Sherman."

"Of course not." Just when I'm having more respect for Dan he says something silly. I walk toward the sink in the room, the only dressing room that even has a sink. "There are two wine glasses in the sink. I assume that means he drank his bottle."

"But an empty bottle could have been used to hit Mr. Padowski on the head."

"Didn't you smell the wine at the crime scene—mixed in with the blood from his head wound?" I wish Officer Prince were here. I'd like to see if her sleuthing skills are more advanced than Officer Daniel's.

"Oh, right. But the bottle could have been half-used."

"Maybe, but I didn't provide a wine stopper, and it's unlikely someone would grab an open bottle of wine if they were planning on hitting someone on the head with it."

"Do you notice anything else unusual?"

"Mario's very large jar of manuka honey is still here," I point to the opened jar that sits on the coffee table next to JJ's name placard.

"What's the point of this manuka honey again?"

"I guess it has antiseptic properties for singers. His assistant had insisted we provide it, though if I'd known he was going to leave the jar here, I'd have told her to tell him to bring his own dang honey. What a waste if this is something he demands at every concert."

Officer Daniel puts on a pair of plastic gloves and pulls a large plastic bag from a briefcase he carries labeled *Property of Tucson Valley Police Department.* "I'll keep your honey safe in evidence just in case, along with the wine glasses," he says as he carefully picks them up and puts them into the bag. "Who else shared this room?" he asks, indicating the two glasses.

"Just JJ."

"Hmm, okay. Let's move on—the room with Mr. Nolan, Mr. Andrews, and Mr. Carson."

I shut off the light to JJ's room and turn the light on in the room across the stage that housed Sunny Moon, Filly Sinclair 2, and Denny Martino. The room looks just as we had left it last night. An empty bottle of wine and three wine glasses sit on the folding table I'd borrowed from my parents' house to furnish the room. Dan collects them for evidence, too. "The baskets are gone, so I assume they've been collected by our performers. There's no way to tell whose bottle they opened."

"Rosi, you have a relationship with these people that I don't have. What do you think about contacting them and asking a few more questions, do a little digging? I think they will be more honest with you."

"I guess I can do that. Like undercover? Will I have to wear a wire?"

Dan laughs, and I feel my face heat with embarrassment. "No, nothing like that. I'm not arresting anyone. I only want more answers—like whose bottle was used, who moved in and out of the dressing rooms, things like that."

"Okay. I can do that."

In Nancy and Elena's room, the plastic flowers I'd left on the TV tray I'd found in the storage cabinet under the stage are gone. I'm glad someone took them. I'd focused on making their room extra pretty. Their gift baskets are gone, too. I notice the full trash can next to the loveseat that had come out of Tracy's office. A crumpled McDonald's bag surprises me as I'd cultivated a nice spread of food donated by Tucson Valley residents. The receipt adjoining the bag says *Nancy*. I tell myself to let it go when I see another slip of paper next to the McDonald's receipt. I pluck it out of the trash.

"What's that?"

"It's some kind of note," I say, handing it over to Dan.

"*I'll meet you after the show,*" he reads. "Who is this for?"

"I don't know. Why would I know that?" Sometimes this man really irritates me.

"I'll take it into evidence." He pulls out another plastic bag from his briefcase and deposits the note inside. "One more room?" he asks.

"Yep, Sherman and Kenny, the Tommy Davis Jr. impersonator, shared a room."

The light is on in the room when we get there. And the room isn't empty. "Kenny?" I ask the startled man who stands before us collecting something into a blue cloth bag.

"Rosi? Officer? Uh, hi."

We wait for an answer.

"I…forgot some things. I came back for them."

"What did you forget?" Officer Daniel points to Kenny's bag.

I can't help but peek inside as Kenny is fumbling for words. "Are those water bottles from the food table?" I ask surprised.

Kenny lowers his head. The normally jovial man with a ready joke looks ashamed and sad. "They are. I assumed that they were up for the taking as you'd provided them for us, and just because we didn't use them all yesterday didn't mean they couldn't still be used. And I took some of the chip bags and power bars, too. I'm sorry, Rosi. I didn't think it would be stealing. And I wasn't even sure I could come back, but when I took a shower in the adjoining sports center last night, I thought I might be able to come back in that way. You caught me." He holds up his hands as if he's ready to be arrested for petty theft.

"Of course those items are free for the taking. They were offered for the performers. And you are one of the finest performers from last night's show." Kenny raises his head until his eyes meet my gaze, and he smiles. "Kenny, I thought you lived locally."

"I do."

"Why did you really take a shower here last night instead of at home?" I squint my eyes, trying to figure out what's not making sense.

"I…I..." Kenny sighs. "I live in a homeless shelter—or with friends."

"Oh!" I don't know how to react. I want to hug him and tell him I'm sorry and that he can take whatever he wants.

"Please don't tell the other performers. They'd never let me perform with them again, and I think I made some real contacts this weekend that might give me some future gigs."

"I won't tell anyone, Kenny. I promise." I squeeze his arm gently. "Take whatever you'd like that's left from last night."

Officer Daniel clears his throat. "Mr. Davis, can you tell us again what you were doing with Mr. Padowski after the show?"

"Sure. JJ brought mugs of hot tea into the room, three of them—for him, Sherman, and me. They had this weird honey in it that JJ swore was supposed to help the throat after singing. It tasted decently. He talked a lot about himself and how everyone loved him. Sherman didn't say much which was kind of odd, if you ask me, cause he was the boastful type, too. Then JJ said something about keeping your enemies close—and I remember this cause he looked right at Sherman, and Sherman looked at his mug of tea which made me look at my mug, too, and I had no idea what was going on. I still don't, but obviously there was nothing in the tea cause I'm still here." He raises his hands as if to say *I don't know?"*

Dan strokes his chin, deep in thought. Or perhaps clueless as to what to make of Kenny's words.

"Did you take your gift basket, Kenny?"

"What? Oh, yeah, thanks, Rosi. That was really nice. Sherman gave me his basket, too, cause he was flying home and all."

"You didn't drink the bottles?"

"Nope. I have them both, back at…well, I have them both. I'm saving them for a special occasion. I also took that pretty flower arrangement. I hope that's okay."

I don't know what Kenny is talking about, but I shake my head up and down, giving silent permission to anything he wishes to take.

"Thanks, Kenny. You've been very helpful," says Officer Daniel as he pats Kenny on the back and leaves the room.

When it's just Kenny and me, I pull out my wallet to give him a twenty-dollar bill.

"No way, Rosi. I'm not taking your money. Things are looking up for me. You paid me for last night, and

Douggy told me about a gig in Phoenix. He's going to ask them to let me perform with him there. I almost have enough money saved up to move in with a friend and pay rent. I'd have my own room, too. No more couch surfing," he laughs uneasily. "Gotta be able to pay my own way. That's important."

"Oh, this isn't charity, Kenny," I say. "A fan of yours gave this to me last night as a kind of tip. She said you were her favorite performer and wanted you to know that you made her night. I just forgot about it after all the chaos of the night."

Kenny's eyes light up. "Really? That's incredible. Thanks." He takes the money and adds it to his bag along with the leftovers from yesterday's food table. "I best get going. Thanks again, Rosi."

"Feel free to use the shower facilities if you want to before you go."

Kenny nods his head in understanding.

It's not nice to lie until it is.

Chapter 13

Mario pops into my office as I am answering the last of my emails. There has been an outpouring of support as well as a lot of theories. Why people in the community have felt the need to write me about their theories instead of telling Officer Daniel and Officer Prince is beyond my comprehension, but I do acknowledge the spread of news in this town as many had discovered the part I'd played in Salem Mansfield's murder investigation. And though I love this new chapter in my life, I miss the investigations and sleuthing I'd do weekly in Springfield. Maybe I can help again with Sherman's case. Plus, it literally happened on the job.

"Hey, Rosi. I checked the cameras as you asked. They weren't on, and I'm embarrassed to say the technology is a bit behind with the system."

I take a slow, deep breath. "Please tell me that the cameras do not use VHS tapes."

"Okay."

"Okay, what?"

"I won't tell you."

I exhale my frustration. "I wish I could say I was surprised. I'll let Officer Daniel know. And I'll ask Tracy for an appropriation of money to update our security systems. What a mess."

"Rosi, don't be too hard on Tracy. She's old school, but her heart for this community is in the right place."

"I know. Thanks for all your help, Mario. Are you doing okay? This hasn't been easy on any of us."

"Celia made me a nice breakfast this morning."

"Good to hear." I wonder again why the women in Mom's social circle dislike her so much. "Go home. It's Sunday. None of us should be here. I'm taking off, too, and Tracy texted that she's leaving in a half hour. We can regroup tomorrow."

"I thought you wanted to put the dressing rooms back in order, return everything to the storage rooms?"

"Tomorrow. We can do that tomorrow. Plus, I'm not sure what I want to do with all of those rooms."

Mario nods his head. "Tomorrow. Yes, that sounds nice. I'll see you then."

I watch Mario walk down the hallway. I don't know if I have ever met a harder working man. I text my realtor and let her know that I'm ready to see some condos and townhouses. It will be a nice distraction. And it's time to move out of my parents' house.

I take Barley to the backyard while I wait for Keaton who will accompany me on my house-hunting adventure. She's doubled in size. I throw a tennis ball across the yard as she chases it in a perpetual game of fetch. "You are a very slobbery beast," I tell her.

"I hope you have nicer things to say to me," says Keaton who opens the gate and lets himself into the backyard.

I laugh. "Well, I guess it depends on how much drool you're producing today."

"I think I'm drooling a bit seeing you in that sundress," he says, pointing to my new sky-blue dress that lands just above my knees. I'm showing more cleavage than usual but nothing like Elena cleavage.

"You're gross," I say, play pushing Keaton away as he comes in for a kiss.

He throws his arms up in the air, "Guilty!"

I let him kiss me this time. Barley barks as she's dropped her ball at my feet, a reminder that she's not to be ignored. I throw the ball a few more times before she tires out and flops onto the cooler concrete on the covered patio. "I guess this means we can go now. Thanks for coming along."

"I wouldn't miss it." Keaton winks at me.

He's not wearing his usual tan khakis and t-shirt. Instead, he's put on a clean green t-shirt with navy blue shorts. He wears new Nikes, and a light scent of aftershave fills the space between us. I find myself moving closer and plant a kiss on his lips, lingering a bit longer than usual.

"What was that for?" Keaton smiles.

"You're a little bit irresistible right now. Sorry!"

"Don't apologize. I'll try to be more irresistible from now on if you're going to act like this." He runs his hands through his thick, dark hair and flexes his arms as if he's in a weight-lifting competition.

I laugh. "Come on. We're going to be late. Safia will be waiting."

"Are you sure we can't be a *little* late?" he winks at me.

"And my dad is watching a documentary on the Great Lakes. Right there. *In the house.*"

"You really need your own place!"

I grab his hand and pull him toward the gate. "I do. Let's go."

Safia, my realtor, is waiting in her car, the engine running for air conditioning, when we pull up to a condo in a neighborhood on the north side of Tucson Valley, a five-minute drive from the retirement community part of Tucson Valley.

She envelops me in a hug the minute she is out of her car, her flowing skirt skimming the top of the driveway. "Rosi, dear, it's so nice to see you again. I was afraid you'd never call me after we last met in my office." She pulls out a scrunchie and knots her long red hair into a side ponytail.

"Things at work have been—complicated," I pause.

"I know! I've thought about you all day. When you called to tell me you had time to see some houses today, I just knew it would be the best therapy for you after what you've been through, you poor thing. House hunting as therapy is a little-known secret. Come along now. Let's get your mind off things." She locks her arm through mine as she leads us to the condo. "Nice to meet you, Mr. Helper," she calls to Keaton from over her shoulder.

"Hello," he says, amused by the woman with the oversized personality. "I'm Keaton!"

She opens the door with the key that's been secured in the lockbox on the door handle. "What we have here is a traditional adobe-style condo with a solid exterior and four units in the building. This unit is on the end, so you only share walls with one other person, though I can assure you that noise does not travel through these walls." She screeches as if to prove her point. She only proves how irksome it is listening to her voice. She adjusts her tortoiseshell eyeglass frames and looks at her phone. "Oh, good news! There's been a five-thousand-dollar reduction in this unit since this morning."

"That's great," says Keaton, though I imagine it's part of a ploy to make me more interested in the condo.

"Maybe I should actually see the unit first," I suggest.

"Poodles! Right this way." She waves her hand across the hallway as if she's a Price is Right model showing off a grand prize.

"What is poodles?" I whisper to Keaton.

He raises his shoulders and throws up his hands.

We walk through an arch entry into the kitchen. I welcome the architectural differences between homes in the Midwest and Arizona. I can appreciate the Southwestern details in this condo like the Earthy tones and the tiles with cacti on the kitchen backsplash, but the condo is tiny. "Are you sure there are two bedrooms in this condo?"

"There are two bedrooms although one of them might be better suited as an office."

I stick my head into the room. "I don't know if there's even room for a twin bed in here."

"Zak might want a little more space," Keaton agrees.

I'd promised Zak that I'd always have a room for him, and he was to consider my new home his as well. I know he's in college now, but college boys need a place to land, even if only for the holidays, and Wes and I had a serious conversation with Zak recently about the holidays and breaks and how we'd work together to be fair with everyone's time. It was one of the most productive conversations I've ever had with my ex-husband.

"There *is* a nice living room space. Perhaps you could get a murphy bed—you know, the kind of bed that pulls down from the wall?"

I shake my head adamantly. "No, that won't do. He needs his own space."

Safia shrugs her shoulders. She steps on the hem of her skirt, stops, and readjusts as I follow her to the owner's suite. "This room is attached to a lovely bathroom."

Keaton sticks his head into the bathroom first. He wrinkles his nose and shakes his head.

"This might have been a lovely bathroom in 1982, but now it's just very brown, so brown that the grout in between the ceramic tiles is the same color as the tiles themselves, and I'm not sure that's the original grout color," I say, echoing his distaste.

"This unit is on the lower end of your budget. Can't your *friend*," she says, pointing to Keaton, "put in a little sweat equity and spiff this bathroom up for you?" She smiles so wide, her dimples appear to slide off her face.

"I could do that, Rosi."

"Nope, nope. I'm not signing you up for anything like that." I check the time on my phone. "Can we see something else, Safia?"

"Sure, moving right along!" She snaps off the condo lights and leads us outside as she hums the music from Britney Spears's "Oops! I Did It Again."

As we follow Safia to the next condo, I stare absently at the Arizona landscape. Keaton could identify every desert plant I am seeing, but I can't. To me everything looks the same—dry. There are no oak trees or maple trees, no daylilies or purple irises. Maybe I'm not cut out to be a transplant. Pick me up and move me back to the Midwest. That's what I know. That's who I am. Can I thrive here?

Keaton puts his hand on my knee. "Are you okay, Rosi?"

I scrunch up my face and massage my temples, the start of a headache coming. "What if I've made a mistake?"

"About Safia? Because I get it. She's a bit much."

"No. I mean, what if I should have gone back to Illinois?"

"Oh. Well, I guess if that's what you really want to do, Rosi, that's what you should do." The features on his face droop simultaneously, and my heart skips a beat.

"Keats, I don't mean that I want to leave you. I love spending time with you. And I like my job. It's just…it's just been *a lot* since I've moved here. It's overwhelming. I've lived in the same home for twenty years. I lived in a 3000 square foot home, and I'm looking at condos that don't even have proper room for my six-foot-tall son. It's a lot to figure out."

"What's most important to you in this home?"

"Having room for Zak—for when he visits—even if it's only a couple of times a year. And I want a view. I want to sit on my back patio or deck and see the mountains in the distance."

"Okay. Then that's what we are going to look for, as long as it takes. You'll find it, Rosi."

"Why are you so good to me?"

Keaton smiles devilishly. "Because one of these days you're going to have your *own* place. Your own bedroom." His entire face lights up with excitement.

I roll my eyes, but the thought of having a sleepover with Keaton is quite appealing.

The next three condos fail to live up to Safia's hype for them. From the renovations needed to the small spaces to the lackluster views to the broken-down fences, nothing screams, *Rosi, this is the place for you.* We are turning back to my parents' street, giving up for the day, when I get a text from Safia.

New listing. Just popped up. I think this is the one, Rosi. Chop! Chop!

"Oh man, Safia has another place she thinks I should see."

"Then let's see it," Keaton says, backing into the closest driveway to turn around.

"I don't know if I have it in me," I say, wishing that the owners of my parents' condo weren't coming back for the summer, and I could rent it out until next fall when they will return, give myself more time for this transition.

Keaton idles the car. "Your call, Rosi."

I look at Keaton who is waiting for my decision. I can't believe I've been so lucky to stumble upon such a patient soul. Wes would have driven straight back to my parents and told me to hire another agent. "Let's go," I say.

This condo is close to work. I can't believe Safia has found a condo just outside the retirement community yet close enough to walk or bike to work.

"Come, come!" yells Safia who is walking so quickly toward the door of the condo that she trips yet again on her skirt. This time she doesn't stop to adjust herself but just hikes her skirt up as she hurries to the lockbox.

"Why the hurry?" Keaton asks.

"Because this condo just came up as a listing! Nothing *ever* opens on this street, and I have it on good authority that there are at least two other agents trying to get their clients over here right now. If you like this place, you need to put an offer in immediately. *Immediately!*"

The urgency with which Safia is talking fuels my adrenaline, and suddenly there is nothing more I want to do than to look at this condo.

She talks so quickly it's hard to follow. "The views, Rosi! The views from this condo are breathtaking. That's why they rarely come up for sale. Many of the homes in the retirement community have the same views, but you have to pay a lot of money to own a home in the retirement community, not to mention the high HOA dues there. This place is much more reasonable—small, for sure—but did I mention the views?"

We follow her into the condo, a lovely mudroom-type area right inside with cubbies to store shoes and hooks for jackets.

Safia pulls the curtains back in the living room with a dramatic flair. She's not wrong. The Santa Rita Mountains stand tall in the distance, the sun setting on the day. No wonder I feel like I've been up for hours. "Gorgeous," Keaton and I say together.

"And there's a little patio back here. Each unit has a small-fenced in area, which will be perfect for Oats."

"Barley," I say.

"Yes, that's what I meant. Now let's look quickly. I can hear the others coming."

Keaton and I look at each other. How does she hear others coming?

"The kitchen is basic, nothing special, but everything you need to cook." She moves on to the bathroom. "There's only one bathroom, but it's a decent size."

"The shower door is falling off," I say, also noticing the outdated bubble lighting above the mirror.

"I can fix that," Keaton whispers so as not to disturb Safia.

"And here are the bedrooms, one on either side of the hallway. What do you think?"

I peek into each of the rooms, equal in size with plenty of room for queen-size beds, a dresser, and a nightstand.

"There's also a small pool and workout room as part of the amenities, and no outside maintenance is needed."

"What's the use in having a landscaper as a boyfriend if he can't do my landscaping?" I say, throwing a look of amusement at Keaton.

"Have him pot some plants," Safia says roughly. "Make an offer, yes?"

Safia's turn in mood is startling. She's been so energized all afternoon; I think she's crashing.

"Well, I…I…"

"Yes?"

"The price is right. The HOA dues are reasonable. The backyard is nice for Barley, and the bedrooms are big enough. I can't beat the commute to work."

"And the views!" interrupts Safia. "The mountains! The *mountains!*"

I look at Keaton. He nods his head and squeezes my hand. "Let's make an offer!"

"Thank the Good Lord up above." Safia pulls out her phone and begins the process.

I shrug my shoulders as if to say *I have no idea what's wrong with this woman.* But I'm happy. I'm genuinely happy. I'm moving to Tucson. My phone rings, a text message awaiting me. I open my phone and read the message.

I know who murdered Sherman.

Now I have to solve a murder.

Chapter 14

Nancy startles me by her appearance. Gone is the wig. Gone are the flashy clothes. Gone are the false eyelashes and layers of makeup. She's stripped down to a plain black t-shirt and black yoga pants. Even her eyes are covered with black sunglasses even though we are meeting at night in her car in the parking lot of the In-N-Out Burger about fifteen miles outside of the retirement community. It's so late that the restaurant is closed, and I hope we don't catch the attention of the local police or someone with malintent.

"Hello, Nancy."

"Hi, Rosi."

"It's kind of a surprise to hear from you. I thought you'd flown back to Vegas."

"Oh that. I was lyin'. I don't have any other gigs scheduled for a few months. I'm not the youngest Martha Franklin out there. Too much competition these days. This morning I checked out of that nice hotel you got for us, and I've been driving my car around town all day, trying to clear my head, figure out what to do. I finally decided to call you 'cause I trust you, Rosi. I know you'll do the right thing."

"The right thing?" I repeat.

"Come here, Rosi."

She whispers so softly that I have to lean over to her side of the car to hear her.

"I think Elena and Sherman were a thing."

"Oh, interesting. And by *thing,* do you mean like casual hookup or serious dating?"

"I don't know," Nancy continues to whisper, "but I found Sherman in our dressing room before rehearsal started, and he and Elena were, uh, not fully dressed."

"Oh!" I say again, processing what to think of this new piece of information. "What happened when they saw you?"

Nancy's eyes get really big. "She flipped. She completely flipped. Sweet little Elena, Star impersonator—she's got a feisty temper."

I try to reconcile what Nancy is telling me with the sweet, gracious woman I met on Saturday afternoon. Sure, she was self-confident in herself, at worst, but when you're playing Star you have to show some confidence, but I never saw any inkling of a temper. "What happened, Nancy?"

"When I walked in on them, like I said, she started screamin' at me to get out, told me to keep my fat mouth quiet or there'd be heck to pay."

"Maybe she was embarrassed. I mean, wouldn't *you* be embarrassed if you were, uh…caught in the act?"

"Sure I would, but I wouldn't scream at the person who walked in on me. But that's not all."

"Go on." I scan the parking lot to make sure that our cars haven't gathered unwanted attention at this hour.

"She didn't just scream at me. She hollered at Sherman, too. She said, "*I told you this was a bad idea. I don't know why I trusted you.*"

"Trusted him about what?"

"I don't have any idea. He pushed himself up, got dressed, and walked out the door without even lookin' at me."

"Nancy," I say softly because her adrenaline flashes from her every pore, "I know this was a disturbing experience, and I understand why you told me. Thank you. But it doesn't mean that Elena *killed* Sherman, right?"

"I don't know, but I'm not takin' any chances." She looks around us, eyes darting like a raccoon caught in the headlights of a pick-up truck on a country road in central Illinois.

"What are you afraid of?"

"Elena didn't talk to me again after that incident—wouldn't even look at me unless there were people around!"

"I had no idea. The two of you seemed to get along so well."

Nancy exhales quickly. "We are actresses, Rosi dear. But Elena holds grudges. I've met women like her. They don't forget."

"Forget what, though? You haven't done anything. You didn't tell anyone about Sherman, did you, except me?"

Nancy drops her head, *guilty* written all over her face with an imaginary stamper.

"Who'd you tell, Nancy?"

"I didn't intend to tell anyone. I was really shaken up, Rosi."

"And?" A couple of people are lingering under the lights at the far end of the parking lot. I'm ready to get out of here. I'm a firm believer in my mother's mantra that nothing good ever happens after midnight.

"I ran into JJ backstage—like, I literally ran into him—and I'm not a small woman. He read my face, asked me to come into his dressing room, and I told him what had just happened."

"What was his reaction?"

"He began pacin' around the room, clenching his jaw, and breathing heavy. It was quite bizarre to be honest. He was mad, really mad."

"That doesn't make any sense. Why would JJ care that Sherman and Elena had been caught in a compromised position? Was he angry that Elena yelled at you?"

"I don't hold that kind of power over JJ," she pauses. "But Elena apparently did."

"What do you mean?"

"Only a man who knows someone *intimately* would care so strongly about what I'd just told him."

"Oh." I let the information sink in. Perhaps Sherman Padowski wasn't the only one enamored with Elena Templeton. "But do you have any reason to believe any of these things caused someone to crack a bottle of wine over Sherman's head and push him off the stage?"

Nancy shudders, her shoulders shaking. "I don't know, but I'm keeping a low profile. That's why I asked to meet you in secret. I'm drivin' back to Vegas tomorrow morning, but I'm stayin' with my mama for a bit, until the police figure this all out. I'm unsettled."

I put my hand on top of Nancy's hand. "It's going to be okay, Nancy. Feel free to reach out any time you want to."

"Thanks, Rosi. Will you let me know if the police make any arrests?"

"Of course I will. Are you okay to go back to your motel tonight?"

She scans the In-N-Out Burger parking lot and spots the same group of people who are hanging out under the lights. "Can you follow me back to my room?"

"Sure. I can do that." I open my car door to go back to my car. "One more thing, Nancy! Don't sell yourself short. You had that crowd rocking. You have a lot of talent."

"Thanks, Rosi dear. You are a sweetie. I'll lead the way to my motel."

After watching Nancy let herself safely into her motel room, I drive back to my parents' house. I tiptoe into the house so as not to wake my parents. Barley barely lifts her head from her snuggly pile of blankets on my bed, some guard dog she'll be when I'm living alone. I tussle her fur, change into my pajamas, and collapse next to her. I don't even brush my teeth.

Chapter 15

"Rosi, can you strip your bed before you leave for work?" asks Mom who is in busy, busy mode as Simon, Shelly, and the kids will be arriving tomorrow from Illinois for their annual Arizona visit.

I wanted an excuse to be busy at work when they got here—too much madness for my liking, three kids under the age of five. But I never dreamed that my excuse would be a murder on the job, and I'm actually wishing I could soak in the chaos of my brother's perfect family (Mom's words) instead of the disorder an unsolved murder at work is causing. "Sure, Mom." I pull the sheets off my bed while Barley thinks I am playing a game of tug-of-war. She pulls on the sheet with her teeth while I try to pry it from her mouth.

Mom sticks her head around the corner of my room. "Do you think Keaton can take Barley for a few days, just while your brother is here? Shelly's worried about the dog being around the baby."

"Barley, you're being replaced," I tease, releasing the bottom sheet from her mouth. "I can ask him. I doubt he'll mind." Mom takes the sheets from me but doesn't leave. "What do you have to say, Mom? Just get on with it."

"I think you should ask Keaton if you can stay with him this week, too, you and Barley."

"Are you kicking me out because beloved Simon will be arriving?"

"Stop this nonsense, Rosi. You sound like a twelve-year-old. Don't be ridiculous. It won't be comfortable sleeping on that couch, and we have one bathroom with three littles, multiple adults, and a father who pees incessantly during the night. I'm thinking of *you*."

I know she's right. And I know Keaton would love to have me stay over. It's the fact that I haven't been with another man in my life except for Wesley that's terrifying me. And even if I truly just *slept* over there, it's a conversation that's coming. I don't know how to handle that pressure. "I'll talk to him, but for now I need to get the performing arts center back in order. We did a lot of rearranging for Saturday's show. We need some normalcy back there."

"Any theories yet?"

"You'd have to ask Officer Daniel."

"I'm asking you, Rosi. I know you know more than you're letting on."

"I don't know much." *And I'm not giving the gossip cluster any ammunition, either,* is what I really think. "I'll see you for dinner. Have fun toddler-proofing the house." I kiss Mom on the cheek, wave goodbye to Dad who is loading his trunk with golf clubs, grab Barley's leash, and put her into the car for what will likely be another very long day on the job.

"Let's keep most of the things we don't think we will need very often in the storage cabinets under the stage," I tell Mario. "Let's put the things we might need, like the folding chairs, back into the room used by Xander, Douggy, and Clyde. We'll maintain the other three rooms for performers or whatever else comes up."

"Sounds good," says Mario. "I can handle that."

"I know you can. But I'm going to help you. I haven't been to the gym since I've been in Tucson Valley. I could use some physical labor to clear my mind, too."

"Okay, I'll meet you in the auditorium when you're ready."

I check my emails before I join Mario. Brenda has sent a message demanding that the retirement community put together a benefit to finance Sherman's funeral. I'm flabbergasted. Who does she think she is? Who does she think Sherman was? And why won't his family pay for his own funeral? I click delete with too much glee.

The first thing I do is remove the personalized touches I'd added to Xander, Douggy, and Clyde's dressing room, the extra furniture I'd found around the center: an oversized beanbag chair, a scuffed-up metal coffee table, the nearly broken folding chair, a fake carnation arrangement, and a set of Arizona landscape paintings I'd hung on the wall. I might be able to repurpose everything into the other dressing rooms, all except for the broken folding chair. I reach for the trash can to empty it when I see one of my gift baskets I'd so carefully cultivated, sitting behind the trash can and hidden from view by the beanbag. I look at the nametag on the basket. It belongs to Clyde. Everything is there, the chocolate, the popcorn, the Tucson pen, the wine glasses, all except for the wine bottle. I make a mental note to tell Officer Daniel after snapping a picture of the basket with my phone.

Nancy and Elena's room takes no time to organize. Everything remains neat and tidy save for a false eyelash on the floor near the vanity table Karen donated when I'd put out a call for gently used furniture. Hers had been the most useful donation. From the thick mascara on the eyelash, I can't tell if it belonged to Elena or Nancy. They both piled on the makeup. I still can't believe that Elena intimidated Nancy so badly that she'd called me out at midnight to tell me her concerns, but I need to let Officer Daniel know about our conversation, too. My list of things to tell him is growing.

My phone dings two times in a row. I fluff up the pillows on the small chaise in the room and shut off the lights before checking my messages.

Since you're paying with cash, closing can be as soon as next Friday. Okay with you? Poodles!

Thanks, Safia. Sounds perfect.

Again, what's with the *poodles?* I still can't believe I'm buying a home in Arizona. I never would have imagined a few months ago when I was still arguing with Wesley about the sale of our house in Springfield that I'd be moving thousands of miles across the country. And the fact that I am downsizing so immensely excites me more than I expected. Doing something so grown up like buying my own condo—and buying my own home with cash because of the crazy valuation of our Illinois home—is icing on the cake. Though our house sale in Illinois won't close until May, Dad and Mom have leant me the money to settle this condo in cash, the sooner the better.

The second message is from Tracy.

Someone here to see you. On her way down. Tried to stop her. Good luck!!

I don't have time to reply when I hear the sound of footsteps walking down the auditorium aisle, someone with dress shoes, heels maybe? I peek behind the stage curtain and see an older woman, maybe in her early 60s, with medium-length red hair that bounces just above her shoulders and matching her ample bouncing chest as she walks with a purpose. She projects an air of importance in her black pencil skirt, button-down white shirt, and peekaboo cleavage. Why do so many women get breast lifts around here?

I step out from behind the curtain, startling the woman who almost drops the pile of papers she grips tightly in her hands. "Hello?" I ask, projecting my best business voice. "May I help you with something?"

"Oh, hi. Yes, you startled me. Are you Rosi, by chance?"

"I am, by chance and by intention," I laugh at my own joke though she does not.

"Good. That's good." She shuffles her papers to her left hand and reaches out her right hand to me. "I'm Dee, Sherman Padowski's assistant."

I walk down the stage steps before shaking her hand. "Hello. I'm…I'm a bit surprised to meet you. Am I to assume that you are the same *Dee* that worked with JJ McMeadows?"

"That's funny," she says with no emotion.

"He said you didn't work for him anymore."

"He did? Hmm…well, JJ has the best sense of humor, doesn't he? I never worked for JJ McMeadows. I can assure you that."

I eye the woman suspiciously. Having a good sense of humor is not a trait I'd have attached to JJ. "What can I do for you, Dee?" I don't have the desire to ask for her last name.

Her mood shifts as she takes in the auditorium, her eyes pivoting from one spot to the next in quick succession. "Is this…where…where it happened?" she asks quietly.

"Oh." I suddenly have compassion for this woman. "Yes. Sherman died in the auditorium. I am so sorry for your loss." I put my hand on her arm, but she pulls away from my touch. "I hope it gives you comfort to know that his last show was spectacular. The crowd loved his Filly Sinclair performance."

She bites her lip and nods her head. "And the other performers?" She arches an eyebrow, awaiting an answer to a question I don't quite understand.

"Yes, everyone was a hit. The whole night was simply amazing until, well…The show was a success."

"I meant, which of the performers murdered my beloved Sherman?"

She says it so matter-of-factly I'm stunned for a moment and don't respond right away. "The police are investigating Sherman's death. I can give you Officer Daniel's number if that would help." I really wish I had another appointment waiting for me so that I could step away from this conversation.

She shakes her head firmly back and forth. "I don't need the police. Sherman told me before he died that you were in charge. You were the one who brought Elena Templeton into the show. So that means that I blame you for Sherman's death. *You* brought that woman back into our lives." She takes a step closer than I like, so I take a step back, hitting the front of the stage with my shoulder.

"I don't know what you are talking about," I say, trying to steady my voice. I reach for my phone in my back pocket and pull it out.

Dee hits my wrist and sends my phone sprawling across the concrete floor of the auditorium. "You don't need your *phone,*" she spits, yet another mood surfacing.

I put out my now open hand, stopping Dee from moving any closer. "You need to leave," I say a lot more calmly than I feel.

"I'm not leaving without Shermy's paycheck."

"Excuse me?"

"You heard me. I am Sherman's assistant. I want his paycheck for Saturday's show."

"I understand how upset and shocked you much be by Sherman's death. I empathize with your situation. However, I never spoke with Sherman about an assistant. I cannot in good conscience give you his final paycheck. I need to abide by what I assume would have been his wishes—to send his earnings to his family. I'm sorry if you don't understand."

Dee's eyes bulge out from her face like she's just shot a metal ball in a pinball machine. "Give me that check!" She drops her papers and grabs both of my wrists with her hands.

"Hey!"

I see Mario out of the corner of my eye running toward us. She sees him, too, and drops her hands as quickly as she'd grabbed my wrists.

"What's going on?" It's the first time I've heard him shout. There's a fear factor in that sound that causes Dee to slink into yet another mood.

"Hello. I'm having a nice discussion with my friend Rosi. Just trying to explain a few things to her that she doesn't seem to understand."

"I understand quite well. I'm sorry for your loss. But it's time to go now. I will make sure to send Sherman's paycheck to his family after I've spoken with Officer Daniel."

"Sherman isn't *married*." Her lips distort at the word *married* as if it's a source of frustration. I can only imagine that Dee may have been interested in more than a work relationship with Sherman Padowski.

"Right, so as I was saying, I'll send the check to next of kin. Mario," I say, turning to make eye contact with him as to say *I've had enough*. "Can you please walk Dee out to her car? I wouldn't want her to get lost." I don't smile. Neither does she.

"This won't be the last of our conversation." She scoops up her papers and walks out of the auditorium ahead of Mario, her air of confidence returning with a mixed bag of defiance and frustration.

When Mario returns, I am sitting on the stage at the opposite end from where Sherman took his final steps. I am trying to imagine why he'd have been so close to the edge of the stage at that moment when everyone else was preparing to sign autographs or—if they didn't want to meet fans—getting ready to leave.

"Wow! She's quite a lady," Mario says, stroking his beard and rolling his eyes.

"I'm not sure a real lady would grab me in a fit of rage like she did."

"Are you okay?" Mario stands in front of me from the auditorium floor.

"I'm fine. Thanks for your help."

"No problem. I think the backstage area is in fine shape, so I'm heading to the aquatic center to do some cleaning. Tracy says they are short-handed today. Do you need anything before I go?"

I don't answer for a second as I contemplate what I want to do next. "Mario, I don't understand why Sherman would have been on the stage at all when everyone else was in their dressing rooms or headed to meet the audience."

Mario shrugs his shoulders. "Maybe someone told him they had a message for him, something they wanted to share in private? Just grasping at straws here."

"Uh-huh. Or maybe Sherman asked someone to meet *him* on the stage."

"You think he asked his own murderer to meet him on the stage?"

"No, of course not. But what if someone else showed up instead?"

"Meaning that the message was passed on for someone else to talk to Sherman for them?"

"Maybe." I tap my teeth up and down, trying to flesh out my thoughts. "Mario, can you stand over there?" I ask, pointing to the stage where Sherman's body must have been before he was pushed.

Mario walks up the stairs from the front of the stage and stands where directed. I walk to the spot where his body landed on Saturday night. I look up at Mario, a good fifteen feet above me. Behind Mario the empty stage looms large. It's hard to imagine such joy on that stage turning to such madness only minutes after the show's end. To the right of where Mario stands now facing me is a door, just offstage and behind the curtain. I'd never opened that door before, but Mario had told me it held additional storage when I'd asked him about it during the frantic hours we'd been searching for more dressing room space. I remember thinking that I needed to do a thorough organization of this place this summer. I climb the same stairs Mario had just climbed and open the door.

"What are you doing, Rosi?"

"I'm not sure yet." Inside the room I reach for a light switch on the wall that is not there.

"There's a pull chain," says Mario who is now standing right behind me.

I reach for a chain and pull it.

"Oh my…"

A pitter patter of mice scurry underneath the metal shelving units when I pull the light, leaving behind what they had not yet carried away from the plates of food that sit on the floor, food from the spread I'd organized for Saturday night's show.

"Why would anyone take their food in here?" Mario asks, picking up the food—plates and all—and depositing them in a garbage can near the door. "And was someone taking a nap?" He points to a pile of pillows and blankets on the floor, the kind of patterned blankets you find in any department store with pictures of dogs or cats or footballs.

"I'm not so sure there was sleeping going on in here," I say, pieces of the puzzle coming together in my mind as I spy a still-flickering battery-operated candle on the floor.

"Oh my," Mario says again. "A love nest?"

"Maybe. And I'm guessing that Sherman may have invited someone to his love nest on Saturday after the show."

"Then why was his body found in the auditorium and not in here?"

"Because maybe somebody else showed up."

Chapter 16

"Aunt Rosi!" A brown-haired boy with curls his mom refuses to cut yet for fear they'll never grow back comes barreling across the living room of my parents' home and into my arms.

"Flynn!" I pick him up and spin him around the room, his four-year-old legs flying out behind him and threatening to take out a picture or two on the wall. Soon his little brother by ten months, Hudson, is grabbing my leg yelling, *"My turn! My turn!"*

I set Flynn onto the couch so he can orient himself before trying to walk after being made drunk with dizziness by Aunt Rosi and repeat the game with Hudson.

"Rosi! You are going to make those boys sick!" Simon, my wiser wise guy brother says as he takes Hudson from my arms and side hugs me.

"Fun sucker!" I say, walking over to Shelly who has just deposited the first baby girl in our family into the welcoming arms of her grandmother. "Hey, Shelly," I say.

Shelly gives me a proper hug. "Hi, Rosi. It's so nice to have you in Arizona when we visit. We can all be a family together here before going back to snowy Illinois. Can you believe that it snowed last week? It's April!"

Apparently, no one, including myself, has yet to tell them that I am not returning to Illinois, at least not on a permanent basis. "Hi, Shelly." I peek into the fluffy pink blanket and see the sweetest plump cheeks and wispy bits of blonde hair—from Shelly. "She's perfect," I say more to myself than to Shelly. I'd always wanted another baby, but Wesley has put his foot down. It wasn't part of *his* plan. I guess I wasn't either as it turned out.

"Isn't she, though?" asks Mom who hasn't taken her eyes off the baby since she'd received her in her arms. "Ten little fingers. Ten little toes. "Ivy, my sweet Ivy."

I look at Shelly. "You're never getting her back this week."

"Well, I am the food source, so I should get *some* time with her." She laughs, an easy laugh that reminds me why Simon fell in love *during* their blind date six years ago. He'd told us the story too many times to count. *Being with Shelly is easy. It's just easy.*

I'd been resentful of his positivity as Wesley and I were at the pinnacle of a challenging marriage when he'd married Shelly. I'd spent the night of their wedding drinking way too much tequila at the bar during the reception and throwing up all over my bridesmaid dress. It wasn't my proudest moment.

Barley sees the commotion in the house, jumping up and down and leaving paw prints on the glass of the slider. Flynn and Hudson run to the door and slide it open before anyone can stop them. "Oh!" Shelly sucks in her breath, reaching for Ivy despite Mom's resistance.

"Down, dog! Down!" yells Simon as he pushes Barley off the boys.

"She's harmless, Simon," Dad tries to reassure him.

I scoop Barley up. She tries to wiggle out of my arms, clearly more interested in the littlest visitors than me. "Can I take the boys outside with Barley and me?" I ask.

Simon looks at Shelly who nods her head in agreement. I don't miss the stage of parenting when you're worried about every possible thing being a harm to your child. I sit on the concrete on the covered patio and try to keep Barley on my lap. "You need to ask the owner before you pet anyone's dog. They aren't all nice like Barley," I tell my nephews.

Flynn's eyes light up with understanding. "Aunt Rosi, can I pet Barley?"

Hudson, idolizing his big brother, repeats in his cutest toddler voice. "Aunt Rovi, I pet, Barwey?"

I smile. "Yes, you may. But don't get too close to her mouth. Pet her back or belly. She loves belly rubs!" As if on cue, Barley rolls onto her back while the boys rub her tummy. There is no one in this backyard who is having more fun than Barley, and there is a lot of joy here right now. Part of me is rethinking my decision to stay with Keaton this week. The chaos of a house full of little kids might be the antidote I need to the craziness at work.

"Tell me, Rosi, what's your new friend like?" Shelly asks as she tosses the salad Mom had created and adds a balsamic vinaigrette.

I watch my dad and mom play with the kids in the backyard as Simon throws Barley her ball which she retrieves eagerly. I can't help but smile. "Keats? He's just a good guy, Shell. I don't know what else you want to know."

"Come on! Don't be so coy. I haven't seen you this happy in years."

"Because I married a man who didn't know how to keep commitments. That has a way of draining the joy."

Shelly squeezes my hand. "True. Well, anyway, I can't wait to meet him for dinner tonight."

"Please keep your husband in line. He can be insufferable."

Shelly grins. "I'll try my best."

The doorbell rings. "I'll get it." I dry my hands on a kitchen towel, smooth down my hair, look at myself in the hallway mirror to make sure my makeup hasn't melted from cooking burgers over the grill, and open the door.

Keaton peeks his head out from around a beautiful bouquet of wildflowers. "Those are beautiful! You didn't need to get me flowers."

Keaton kisses me on the cheek. "Don't worry. I didn't," he grins. "The flowers are for your mom."

"Oh! Good call. Come on in—ready or not!" Keaton follows me to the backyard where Shelly has joined her family.

"Keaton!" Mom picks Hudson off her lap and sets him on the ground where Barley proceeds to lick his sockless toes. She greets Keaton with a hug and accepts his bouquet. "These are gorgeous! Thank you! Do you see these flowers, Richard? Perhaps you could learn a thing or two from Keaton."

Dad hangs his head, shaking it back and forth, 'Way to go, Keaton. You make me look bad, man."

Keaton holds up his hands. "Sorry about that. No harm intended. I'm trying to score points with that other lady, too," he says, pointing at me.

"You scored points with me!" Shelly reaches across the table to shake Keaton's hand as she holds the sleeping beauty queen. "I'm Shelly."

Keaton shakes her hand. "Nice to meet you, Shelly."

After all of the introductions have been made and Keaton and Simon have finished a game of tag with Flynn and Hudson, Dad takes the burgers off the warmer on the grill, and we follow him inside where Shelly and I have set the table. Simon sets Hudson in an elevated seat so that he is closer to the table. Flynn beams as he realizes he's big enough to sit at the table like all the grown-ufs, as Hudson calls the rest of us. Shelly puts Ivy into her portable bassinet. Ivy is wearing a Golden Girls' onesie. Mom couldn't help herself. Barley watches us all sadly from the other side of the slider.

"Tell us about work, Simon," Dad says as puts two deviled eggs onto his plate.

"It's good. My senior app is number one in the Apple store for its demographic."

"Does that mean you're making lots of money now?" asks my less-than-tactful mother.

Simon laughs. "Is that what matters, Mom?" He gives her a sly smile, though, so her question still receives its answer.

Simon measures his success by the amount of money he's making, the size of house he lives in, the number of kids he creates. He's always been the basketball captain, the student council representative, the fraternity president. There's never been a competition he hasn't won—including the rivalry for my parents' attention; but as I listen to Simon explain his business and how it helps someone other than himself, I'm impressed. And a new idea percolates in my brain that I file away for another day.

"I think that's incredible that this application can help seniors to get the resources they need more quickly and efficiently. That's wonderful, Simon."

"We call it an *app,* Mom, not an *application.* I want you to have all the details correct when your gossip group gets together next."

I nearly spit out my water because he is so right. There's nothing Mom loves more than to brag on her kids. I've felt that since I've been here, and maybe having my parents to myself without Simon's family being in the same town taking their attention has improved our relationship, too.

"I'll ignore that comment," Mom says lightheartedly, "but let me tell you about Brenda! She's been a mess since Sherman Padowski died."

"Who is Sherman Padowski?" asks Shelly as she cuts up Hudson's hamburger.

"Isn't that the guy who died at your work, Rosi?" asks Simon.

"Yes. After Saturday night's show, someone smashed a wine bottle over his head and pushed him off the stage."

Shelly shoots me a look as if to remind me that there are young children at the table. It's been a long time since I've had to censor myself at a dinner table.

"That was a crazy *joke*, wasn't it?" Keaton asks, saving me from myself.

"Oh, yeah, what a silly thing to do. That's not what nice people do, right, Keaton?"

He shakes his head. "Nope, nice people are *nice* to each other because that's what they are supposed to do." He smiles so big I have to stop myself from laughing as everyone looks at Hudson and Flynn who seem completely uninterested in anything we've said in the last few minutes. Ah, kids—to be so young and naïve, but Shelly seems satisfied with our cover.

"Anyway," says Mom, choosing her words more carefully, "According to Jan who told Paula who told Karen who told me, Brenda may have been more than just a referral for Sherman's participation in the show."

"Huh?" asks Simon.

"Brenda's cousin's wife's brother was Sherman Padowski," I say, as if that will clear anything up. I stifle a giggle.

"Brenda had a thing for Sherman. She sent him flowers before the show."

"Oh! Those must be the flowers that Kenny took," I say to myself.

"Why'd she send him flowers?" asks Shelly.

"Karen said that Paula said that Jan said that Brenda said that she met him when visiting her cousin last summer at a family party and that he flirted with her—even in front of George—and that made him so jealous that they had to leave the party early. But Brenda was so turned on by the experience that she'd tried to figure out how to get to see him again, and when Rosi started planning this '60s extravaganza, she knew just how to make that happen!"

"Well, I hope she's happy because now the man's dead," I say matter-of-factly."

"Rosisophia Doroche Laruee! That's a terrible thing to say," says Mom, but Simon defends me.

"It's your fault for naming her after the Golden Girls because that's exactly what more than one of those women would have said."

Keaton takes another hamburger as the plate is passed around the table. "Renee, are you suggesting that George kil…uh, did a mean thing to Sherman out of jealousy?" he asks.

Shelly smiles at his covert use of vocabulary. I admire the muscles that protrude under the sleeves of his red polo shirt and find myself wishing we were alone.

"I'm not suggesting anything," she says coyly. "Just sharing what I know."

"Renee, stop it with the veiled accusations. George may be a jealous man. But he's not a…"

At that moment, baby Ivy starts crying, the cry of a hungry baby. Shelly jumps up from the table to feed her, and conversations return to more mundane, everyday topics, though I can't forget the memory of finding George and Brenda in the auditorium at the same time I saw Sherman's dead body resting on the cement floor.

Chapter 17

I collapse onto Keaton's couch in his condo after leaving my parents' house after the boys had fallen asleep. They would have thrown a fit if they knew we were leaving.

"Did you ever consider having children when you were married? Because you are so good with those boys." Barley jumps on my lap, Keaton's cat Ruthie running behind the television. Poor kitty. Barley is *a lot*.

Keaton opens a beer can and hands me a glass of white wine. He sits in the easy chair across from me. "That's a complicated question."

"Sorry. It's none of my business."

"It is your business, so long as *I'm* your business," he smiles, melting my heart a little bit more.

"My ex-wife and I wanted kids from the beginning of our marriage, but she never got pregnant. So, we went through some testing, and apparently, I have a low sperm count."

"Oh. Okay."

"We investigated using a sperm donor—from one of those sperm banks, nothing weird."

I take a long sip of my wine.

"And then my mom died, and I kind of lost my will. I was angry. I wasn't fun to be around, and I didn't want to think about bringing a baby into the world that my mom wasn't a part of anymore. Our marriage went downhill for many reasons. Then we got divorced. She remarried a year later and has twins that are two years old now."

"Wow. How do you feel about that?"

Keaton shrugs his shoulders. "I'm happy. I really am." He sets his empty beer can on the coffee table. "But I'd be lying if I didn't tell you that I have some regrets."

I shake my head in agreement. I'd always wanted a sibling for Zak, but at least I had Zak, and I can't imagine a life without him. I'm also sad because Keats should be dating a woman that can give him a child. I have no desire to add to my family *now* at almost forty, even if it were possible, as I'd had to have a hysterectomy two years ago.

Keaton gets up and sits down next to me on the couch. "Why the sad face, Rosi?" He tips up the bottom of my chin so that I am looking into his eyes.

"You should have kids," I say quietly.

"What?" He twirls my hair around his fingers.

"I think you should have kids—marry a woman that can give you the family you regret not having."

Keaton laughs. "You are a silly girl, Rosi."

"But I'm not. You admitted that you have regrets. I don't want you to look back at some point and regret your time with me when you could be building a family with someone that wanted one. There are better medical treatments now. I'm sure doctors could help you and your wife to have a baby."

"My wife?" He gives me a quizzical look.

"Your new wife."

"I don't have a new wife. And if I ever choose to get married again, I'm not at the same place in my life that I was when I was married before. I'm at peace with not having kids. I don't want kids *now*."

"You don't?"

Keaton shakes his head back and forth adamantly. "Did you not see how exhausted your brother and Shelly were? I don't want that anymore. That's why I have Ruthie. She's my baby." He points to the cat who has now jumped onto the dining room table, keeping a watch on Barley who snores on my lap. "And now I have Barley, too." He pats my dog on the head before pulling me close and putting his arms around my shoulders. Barley scampers to the beanbag chair on the floor.

I have never felt so wanted in my life as I do right now. I let myself be fully present in the moment as Keats and I kiss on the couch in his condo.

"Have you thought about where you might sleep tonight?" Keaton asks as he pauses for a moment, my heartbeat matching his in speed.

"Oh! I thought I was staying here," I say, pulling away.

Keaton pulls me back. "I mean, do you want the couch or do you want my bed?"

I feel my face flush as the heat rises up my neck. "I…I…"

Keaton smiles. "Please say you want my bed."

"I want your bed," I whisper because I've never wanted anything more than I do at this moment, and I let him pick me up and carry me into his room, moving our relationship to a whole new level. Life is good.

After showering, which took on a whole new meaning this morning when Keaton pulled back the curtain, I get dressed for my trip to Phoenix with Officer Daniel. We are making a surprise visit to see JJ McMeadows in concert at a casino. He'd been avoiding all of Officer

Daniel's calls, emails, and text messages, so Dan asked me if I wanted to come along for the ambush, as he's calling it.

"Are you sure it's okay if I keep Barley here today? Ruthie might revenge pee outside the litter box," I say as I slip on a pair of shorts.

"I'll keep her in my room. She'll just have to get used to Barley."

"Really? Do you think I'm staying here more than the couple of days my brother and family are in town?" I smile seductively, a new look that feels good on me.

"I hope so." He plants a giant kiss on my lips, and I linger as long as I can before I have to leave to meet Dan at the station.

"I'll see you tonight. Have a good day at work."

"It's only 90 degrees today. There's a chill in the air."

"I'm surely going to melt this summer."

"Nah, it's an excuse to ditch your clothes."

I slug him playfully, refill Barley's water bowl, and put my phone in my purse before leaving. "Be good."

"Aren't I always?"

Keaton's wink is the last thing I see as I walk out the door of his condo into the brilliant sunshine of a new day of possibilities.

Chapter 18

Officer Daniel wears a pair of chino shorts and a blue button-down shirt with pink flamingos. If he's trying to fit in with the retiree crowd at JJ McMeadows's casino concert, I think he's nailed the look. He's driving his personal car today as he says we may have to do a little undercover work if JJ doesn't cooperate. I'm grateful for the invite. The write-ups in the local press and online nationwide about the murder at Tucson Valley Retirement Community Performing Arts Center are killing our reputation—pun intended. He needs to solve this mystery—and quickly. Tucson Valley Retirement Community consistently ranks in the top ten best retirement communities in the nation. The more homes that are sold here, the more money the senior center gets to spend on awesome opportunities such as expanding the sports center, bringing in experts to teach hobby classes, and offering high-quality programming at the performing arts center. When a performer dies under your watch, the interest in the retirement community dies, too.

During the hour and a half trip, Dan talks about Officer Prince and her apparent ineptitude when it comes to police work. "She comes to work late. She's so concerned about hurting someone's feelings that she won't even write a parking ticket! The number of complaints I'm getting from people illegally blocking driveways and parking in business lots when they're not fraternizing the businesses is getting out of hand. Not to mention the fact that she can't string together a sentence to save her life. Her written reports are horrendous. They look like something a fourth grader would write—and that's being too cruel to fourth graders!"

"Then why'd you hire her?" It seems like the most logical question.

"County sheriff's niece."

"Oh, gotcha. That reminds me. Now this is *purely* gossip. I can't make that any clearer, but can I assume you've ruled out George and Brenda Riker from any wrongdoing in Sherman's death?"

"What's the gossip, Rosi?" He glances at me quickly before returning his eyes to the road.

I sigh because I want to be part of the solution, not part of the problem, but in the small chance that any of Jan's/Paula's/Karen's/Mom's gossip is true, it's worth a mention. "Perhaps Brenda had a bit of a crush on Sherman.

She'd met him at her cousin's house before and may have felt like he was giving off some signals."

"Signals?"

"Of the *I'm hot for you* kind. And George whipped up an attitude hotter than a batch of mashed potatoes, as Grandma Kate used to say."

"Good old jealousy—another positive motive for murder?"

"Possibly?"

"I can put that rumor to bed, as *my* Grandma Tilda used to say," he grins. "At least three witnesses saw George and Brenda walk into the auditorium within a minute of hearing Brenda start screaming when she saw Mr. Padowski's body."

"Both of them?"

"Both of them."

"That's good. Mom will be happy to hear that."

"She might want to reconsider her friends, though. That lady has been a thorn in my family's side since my parents were on the HOA board with her years ago."

"Why did your parents leave Tucson Valley?"

"Honestly, they got fed up with the politics that exist here. Don't get me wrong. It's a great place to live. My parents loved it, and I still live in their house. That's part of the problem, though. They are still listed as the owners because I'm not 55 and am not supposed to be living here. The new board has made an exception since I'm a police officer in Tucson Valley. I provide extra security for the retirement community when necessary, free of charge in exchange for the exception, but not everyone is happy about it. Brenda always knows someone who knows someone that wants to buy my parents' house and kick me out. I wish she was a snowbird and flew home for the summer."

"That stinks."

"Do you have any other theories? Besides Brenda?"

"Off the record?" I ask, watching the barren desert landscape outside the window of the car as we travel along Interstate 10.

"Okay."

I tell him about my meeting with Nancy in the In-N-Out Burger parking lot and her fear of Elena after catching her with Sherman.

"That's some important news," he says angrily. "Don't you think you should have told me that earlier?"

"It was a recent conversation. You weren't there, Dan. She was really scared."

"I can understand wanting to keep a torrid affair with a murder victim a secret—I suppose—but not from me. I need to ask her some questions, figure out if she knows more than she's let on."

"I think that's a good idea. But there's more."

I watch Dan tighten his grip on the steering wheel, wondering why he's often the last one to know the important information about this case. "Go on."

"Nancy said she ran into JJ after her encounter with Elena and told him what she'd seen."

"I thought you said she was afraid of Elena?"

"You do stupid things when you're scared? I don't know why she told him, but she said JJ's reaction was strange."

"How so?"

"She said his face turned red, and he swore under his breath."

"Interesting."

"Maybe you can ask JJ about his relationship with Elena? I don't know of any connection between them. In fact, it seemed like they'd only just met on Saturday."

"Rosi, do me a favor, okay?"

"Sure," I say as we turn into the parking lot of the Winding Path Casino. JJ McMeadows's picture flashes on the marquee announcing his show tonight. The picture they use must have been taken after his last Botox injection.

"Let me ask the questions."

"Understood." I hide my smile by turning my head toward the window. This man's ego is so fragile. It would just be cruel if he saw my real thoughts.

The casino is, as are most casinos in the country, teeming with people. At this time of day—late in the afternoon on a Thursday—the clientele mimics the population of Tucson Valley Retirement Community, though there are still plenty of people in their 20s-50s, too. Smoking has been banned in this Arizona casino, I notice, which makes this visit more palatable to my eyes which sting when I am anywhere there is too much smoke. I can't even toast marshmallows over a campfire without suffering the effects of blowing smoke. I'd spend a half hour coughing even after the fire was doused. Dad gave up on including me on camping trips by the time I was in middle school, and weekend excursions in our four-man tent became a father/son activity.

Officer Daniel talks with someone in security while I observe the people playing slots. Gone are the days of pulling the arms on a slot machine, replaced with the simple push of a button. Wesley had won $500 pulling that slot arm early in our marriage. Of course, he'd blown it all on the craps table. He'd blamed *me* for not being "hot" when I blew on his dice before he threw them. Now I've felt like I've won the jackpot after getting out of that marriage.

"JJ is in the back. Ready to pay him a little visit?" he grins evilly. "Let's show him what happens when he thinks he can ignore my calls and messages." He makes a fist and pounds it into his other hand, symbolically socking it to him, I guess.

"I'm ready."

"Here. Put this badge around your neck. *Security.*"

"Cool."

Someone with a security badge pinned to his jacket and not just looped around his neck swipes a keypad on the wall. The door opens and we are directed to follow the hallway to the end, turn right, and choose dressing room number 2 where we will find JJ McMeadows. My heart races as we walk down the hall, much as it used to when I'd been led into the county jail to interview a tarnished politician who'd ended up in lockup. That happened more times than one would imagine.

A plastic nameplate with JJ's name marks his door. It is much more official looking than the paper nameplate I'd made last minute when I'd been forced into finding space for all eight of our performers. I can't believe that was only a week and a half ago.

Dan takes a deep breath and closes his eyes for a moment before knocking on the door. I try to telepathically send him courage.

"Come in, sweetie," we hear from the other side of the door.

I shrug my shoulders. "Go ahead," I whisper.

Officer Daniel turns the doorknob and walks into JJ's dressing room. He is sitting on a chaise lounge, the color of a gold nugget bar. Smoke circles float through the air, his back to us. I guess the no smoking rule only applies to gamblers, though I'm surprised the smoke alarms don't go off. "Come stand over here so I can see you, baby," he says seductively.

I try not to laugh as Dan nods his head at me and points toward JJ. This is more fun than I thought it would be. I walk toward the chaise, but I'm immediately caught up in the ill effects of the perfectly formed smoke circles and begin coughing. So much for a surprise.

"What the hell?" JJ jumps up from his chair, catching sight of both Dan and me. "What…what are you doing here?"

Dan sticks out his hand and retracts it in one motion. Smooth. "I'm Officer Dan Daniel with the Tucson Valley Police Department. I think you might recognize my name from the dozens of messages I've left for you, Mr. McMeadows. And this is Rosi Laruee."

I raise my hand, "Hello again, JJ."

"What do you want?" JJ enunciates the *t* in the word *want*. "I don't know anything. I didn't answer your questions because I have nothing to add to the narrative about Mr. Padowski's death. It would not only be a waste of my time but also of yours."

"Let me decide the value of what you have to say. Seeing that you don't perform until tonight, can I assume that you have a few minutes to answer those questions now?"

JJ looks at his Apple Watch. He pulls out his phone and sends a message to someone I assume to be *sweetie*. No time for a booty call now. "I've got a few minutes."

"Great. Do you mind if we sit down?" He points to a set of matching chairs across from his chaise that complement the color with flecks of gold scattered throughout.

"Fine."

Dan pulls out his notepad. "I want to know about your relationship with Mr. Padowski."

"My relationship? I never met the man before Friday's rehearsal. Next." He rotates his pointer finger in the air.

"What did you do immediately upon leaving the stage after the concert?"

JJ runs his hands through his perfectly coifed hair and takes a deep breath before answering. He truly looks many years younger than his age. "I met my fans."

"Can you elaborate?"

"I signed autographs in the hallway for my adoring fans, where the other performers were also doing the same thing. I was the only one who earned their popularity with original talent, not that impersonator fakery. My line was, by far, the longest, of course."

Dan looks at me, and I nod in agreement. It was the longest line. "What about right after the show?" I ask.

"What do you mean? I imagine I threw some water on my face, put on a fresh shirt, that kind of thing."

"Mr. Davis told me that you had brought green tea and manuka honey into his and Sherman's dressing room after the show."

"Oh, well, yeah. I did that. I forgot."

"Why did you do that, Mr. McMeadows?"

"I don't know. I'm a nice guy." He throws up his hands and shrugs. "Manuka honey soothes my throat. Rosi gave me a gigantic bottle, so I figured I'd share with Kenny and Sherman."

I want to tell him that the least he could have done was to thank me for providing all of his silly requests.

"Did you really have time to drink a cup of tea before meeting your *adoring fans* as you call them?"

"It was a quick cup, but it did the trick, gave me a strong voice to meet with concertgoers, sign autographs, and take pictures. I'm sure you'll find a lot of those pictures on social media. I can pull them up for you if you'd like." He pulls out his phone to open his accounts.

"There is no need to show me. Rosi agrees that you were with fans. Did Mr. Padowski share words with you or Mr. Davis?"

"Words?"

"Did you have any kind of disagreement or perhaps overhear one?"

"Not at all. We drank our tea, shared our mutual positive assessment of the concert, and parted ways."

"And when was the last time you saw Mr. Padowski?"

"In his dressing room, like I just told you. Look, this was a wasted trip for you. I told you I didn't have anything to add. I'm sorry. Really, I am. I need to prepare for my show now. Okay?"

Dan looks defeated. There was no big reveal. We are no closer to discovering who murdered Sherman.

"Thank you for your time, Mr. McMeadows, although you could have saved us all a lot of trouble if you'd answered my questions when I first reached out."

JJ doesn't answer.

When we are back in the casino, I know I need to do something to cheer Dan up, or he's going to spiral quickly. Poor guy. "Let's get dinner. On me! There's a great steak place I read about on Tripadvisor while in the car. What do you say?" I put my hand on his shoulder. "Steak on my dime?"

He smiles slightly. "Thanks, Rosi. I know what you're doing. I'll eat an early dinner with you, but it's my treat. I'm the one that asked you to come all this way with me—for nothing."

"I wanted to come. My treat, but you leave the tip. Come on. Let's see if we can get the early bird special since I'm paying."

We walk to the restaurant which is near the entrance to the casino. I'm reading the specials on the menu on the sign outside the restaurant while Dan puts in our name with the hostess. I can't believe there's a wait this time of day, but I guess there is no concept of time in a casino for a reason. Just as I'm trying to decide whether I want the filet mignon or prime rib, something familiar catches my attention out of the corner of my eye. It catches Dan's attention, too, as he returns to my side. The hair. The body. The attitude with which she walks.

"Would you look at that?" he says, shaking his head.

"Are you thinking what I'm thinking?"

"Yep, I sure am. We know who sweetie is now."

"We sure do."

Chapter 19

Without another word, we ditch our steak dinner idea to follow Elena Templeton through the casino. We stay back a few paces, using the massive banks of slot machines and gaming tables to give cover. Her long black hair is unmistakable, slinking along the back of her skintight jumpsuit. She garners looks from everyone she passes. Even when not performing she truly bears a striking resemblance to Star. She speaks with the same security person that Dan had spoken to a couple of hours ago. He walks with her to the same door that leads to the same hallway and to JJ McMeadows's dressing room.

"Do you think it means anything, Elena being here—with JJ?" I ask.

"I don't know, but that story you shared about Nancy feeling threatened by Elena because she caught her with Sherman followed by her perception of Mr. McMeadows's reaction when she told him gives me enough reason to question him further—and Ms. Templeton."

"I agree."

Dan and I look at our badges, still hanging around our necks. I nod a silent *yes*. My heartrate rises much as it did when I rode with the Illinois State Police when they arrested the most infamous money launderer in the state's history. Dan puts his Officer Daniel persona back on as he talks to the same security guard—again. He swipes the keypad, and we are back in the hallway to pay another visit to JJ McMeadows and his sweetie.

We pause at the door outside his dressing room. I put my ear to the door like I used to do when Simon and his high school girlfriend were in his bedroom. There'd been a strict *no door closed* rule in the house when friends of the opposite sex were over, but Simon was the first to break that rule when my parents were out of the house. If only they knew the rules my perfect brother broke without their knowledge. I wonder why I never ratted him out.

I can hear talking though I can't make out what they are saying. Dan knocks on the door. No one says a word. He knocks again. The door opens slightly. JJ's eyes widen with surprise when he sees us standing in front of him again.

"Look, I told you I don't know anything. You're harassing me at this point."

"Oh, my bad," says Dan, holding up his hand. "I'm not here to talk to you, Mr. McMeadows. I'm here to speak with Ms. Templeton."

That's my cue to push the door open further. Dan and I pass by JJ before he knows what is happening. Elena lies draped on the same chaise lounge JJ had laid on earlier when he'd been perfecting his smoke circles, a blanket draped across her lap.

"Officer Daniel? Rosi? What are you doing here?"

"Good day, Ms. Templeton. It's nice to see you again."

She doesn't say a word as she looks between the three of us, trying to make sense of the situation.

"You see, we still have some questions about Mr. Padowski and his unfortunate demise."

"Yes, of course. I told you everything I knew back in Tucson. What more do you need to know?"

"Well, I guess you can start by telling me more about your relationship with Mr. Padowski."

"I met Sherman the same day I met everyone else."

"Is it normal for you to, uh, unclothe yourself within hours of meeting someone?" I ask as delicately as possible.

"What?" A simultaneous look of horror and understanding passes across her face.

I give her my best *I know about what you did* look.

"This is ridiculous!" JJ yells, causing all of us to jump in surprise. "This is harassment!"

"You have quite a temper, Mr. McMeadows," says Dan. "Might that temper have flared a wrath of jealousy when you found out that Ms. Templeton was also seeing Mr. Padowski?"

JJ freezes midstep on his way to pour himself a stiff drink at his dressing room bar. He turns around slowly. "I…how…"

Elena stands up. "It's true," she says dramatically. "I had a brief relationship with Sherman, but I realized during the weekend in Tucson that he wasn't the man for me."

"Was that before or after he was murdered?" I ask, perhaps a bit too snidely.

"That is uncalled for!" JJ slams his fist on the bar, making his newly poured drink splash over the edge of his glass.

"It was before," Elena says quietly.

"And when did the two of you begin a relationship?" Dan asks, looking at Elena for an answer as JJ rages in the corner of the room.

Elena sighs. "JJ and I go way back from my early days in the industry. I was a back-up singer in my early 20s. He saw my potential, got me a few gigs. I will always be grateful to him." She looks admiringly at JJ who untenses his fists as he looks at her.

The fact that there's likely a thirty-year age difference between Elena and her paramours isn't lost on me, and though JJ holds a certain charm for his audience when he's performing, there isn't much about him offstage that's appealing. He's vain and self-centered with a clear temper. I really want to ask Elena *why*, but I don't get the chance.

"Mr. McMeadows, you're needed for warm-ups on stage," a young woman says, peeking her head into the room, surprised to see so many people occupying the small space. "I also brought the jar of manuka honey you requested." She sets the jar on the coffee table. Why doesn't he bring his own dang jar? What a waste.

"To love a woman is not a crime, Officer Daniel," says JJ. "Perhaps you should try it sometime. It might loosen you up a bit." He slams the door behind him, leaving Elena, Dan, and me alone.

"You need to leave," she says softly. "You've caused enough harm here today. JJ is a gentle, protective man. You have no idea how much he cares for people."

"Does he care enough to kill?" Dan asks.

Her face contorts from sweetness to fury in seconds. "Get out of here!"

"I'll be in touch," he says, turning toward the door.

I follow him. "Enjoy the show tonight." I don't get a response.

"There's another person I need to talk to again, Rosi. Do you mind?" asks Dan as he drives out of the casino parking lot. "I need to make a call to Mr. Andrews."

"Can you call him now?" I am way too invested in this case to leave all the sleuthing to Officer Daniel.

"I was hoping to. Do you have his number by chance? My information is back at the station."

"I think I have his number in my contacts." I pull out my phone and scan through my contacts. Clyde's number is listed as Sinclair 2 in my phone, perhaps an unfair label that led him to rage kill Sinclair number 1.

I push the numbers on my phone and push the speaker button so that Officer Daniel can do the talking.

"Hello?" says a gruff voice from the other end of the line, probably thinking a telemarketer is calling.

"Hello, Mr. Andrews?"

"Yes?"

"This is Officer Daniel from Tucson Valley. We met the night of your performance."

"Oh, yeah. I remember. What can I do for you, sir?" he asks, his voice softening.

"It's come to my attention that the door next to the stage was exit only."

"Okay. So, what does that have to do with me?"

"You had a contentious relationship with Mr. Padowski," Dan states matter-of-factly.

"I certainly did. But just because you don't like a guy doesn't mean you murder him if that's what you are implying."

"I'm not implying anything, just looking for some answers. And one of the questions I need answered is, what were you *really* doing immediately after the show ended? Because it wasn't smoking outside. You would not have been able to get back into the auditorium through that door.

A long pause carries loudly through the phone line. "It's true. But it's not what you are thinking. I couldn't say it in front of that lady that was running things…"

"Rosi?" Dan asks while looking at me.

"Yeah, I couldn't say the truth in front of Rosi and the others about what I was doing."

"Go on."

"I was puking my guts out. That Sherman guy had me so torn up inside all week in a heated competition for number one Filly Sinclair singing rights that I made myself sick. I didn't even make it to the curtain call where all the entertainers took their bows. I barely made it to the bathroom in time."

I quickly pull out my phone and scroll through pictures. Sure enough, Clyde Andrews is not in the pictures of the curtain call, his absence not even missed. It's actually pretty sad. I nod my head at Dan and point to my phone.

"Thank you, Mr. Andrews. You've been a big help. And for what it's worth, Rosi told me you were her favorite singer of the night."

"Really?" he asks, the first hint of joy in his voice.

"Really," he lies.

And I don't mind at all.

It's after dinner when we get back to Tucson. Dan and I had talked the entire trip about our theories regarding JJ and Elena. We hypothesized every which way about whether one of them or both of them had killed Sherman and if jealousy were enough of a motive to cause someone to kill in such a brutal manner. No matter how many hypotheses we had, though, there was zero proof that either one of them had wielded the fatal wine bottle.

I knock softly on Keaton's door. We aren't yet at the *I need a key to your place* stage, although after last night I'd say we are one step closer. He's wearing boxer shorts, and his hair is astray as if he'd been asleep.

"I am so sorry! Were you sleeping?"

He grins sheepishly. "Just a little nap. Sorry. I'm not used to being seen in my everyday man attire."

"Don't apologize. I like it. I like it *a lot*." And I pull him back into his bedroom and forget all about Sherman Padowski.

Closing is still on for next Friday.

I turn down the volume on my phone after Safia's text wakes me up.

Keaton rolls over to face me, his hair even more disheveled than last night. "Has Dan given you any updates?" he asks.

"No. Sorry about that. I forgot to put my phone on *do not disturb*."

He grabs my hand as he stares at me from his pillow. "I'll forgive you. I think you may have been a bit distracted."

He smiles, and I must resist an intense desire to shimmy out of my panties again. "No. It was Safia. I'll be the owner of my very own condo next Friday."

"Aw, that's too bad," he says teasingly.

"I can't stay here, at least not permanently—though, don't get me wrong—it's been fun." I squeeze his hand. "Baby steps."

"Whatever you say, Rosi. I'm just going to enjoy this little playdate while your brother's family is in town." He throws the sheet off his body and gets out of bed, walking toward the bathroom.

I laugh. "I think you forgot something," I say, holding up his boxer shorts which are still lying in the bed.

When Keaton's dressed for work, he joins me in the kitchen for eggs and toast, an uncomplicated breakfast for an uncomplicated man. "Are you free to join us for dinner tonight? Simon, Shelly, and the kids are flying back to Illinois tomorrow."

"Yeah, I'm looking forward to it. I told Flynn I'd bring my frisbee."

"That sounds fun. I really appreciate you wanting to be with my family." I take a long drink of my coffee as I watch him eat his eggs.

"I love your family."

"Me, too."

"And I'm a little more than crazy about you, Rosisophia Doroche."

"As am I about you, Alex P. Keaton."

We kiss over our Americana breakfast until my coffee's gone cold—coffee breath and all.

Chapter 20

I drive straight to my parents' house from the senior center, so I am not late for dinner. It's the last night Simon, Shelly, and the boys are in town, and I've been busier than expected this week because of my outings with Officer Daniel. Plus, our next event—a local barbershop quartet we've added to the schedule to bring some positivity back to Tucson Valley—will be performing in three days. It's the first show since Sherman's murder, and people are understandably nervous about attending. Officer Dan has assured me that he and Officer Prince will provide security to help put everyone's minds at ease, especially the gentlemen who will be singing.

Keaton's car is already parked in front of the house. That means that Barley is here, too, which I am sure thrills the boys—but Shelly—not so much.

"Aunt Rosi!" Flynn flings his arms around the bottom of my legs while Hudson steps on my feet and hugs me at the knees. It reminds me of the days when Zak would hang on my legs when I'd been trying to wash dishes whining, *Mama play. Mama play.* I wish now that I'd let the chores go and sat on that floor and played more.

"Hey, guys. Nice to see you, too."

I hug my Dad who is holding Ivy on his lap in his recliner. Mom and Shelly are in the kitchen while Simon keeps pushing Barley off the couch. Keaton picks her up and gives me a kiss on the cheek. "Hello, beautiful," he whispers in my ear. My heart quickens a little every time he is near.

"Dinner!" Mom yells from the dining room.

"I sit by Keaton!" says Flynn.

"No, I do!" says Hudson.

"Well, lucky for you, Keaton has two sides, one for each of you," Shelly says. She attaches Hudson's booster to a chair next to Keaton, and Flynn sits on the other side. I choose a seat across the table next to Simon and Shelly while Mom and Dad take the heads of the table. It's been a long time since our family looked so complete around a dinner table, except for the other night, of course. I miss Zak and wish he weren't so far away, but already Keaton and Simon get along better than he and Wesley ever did. Wesley wasn't a techie and never cared to know what new idea was swirling around inside my brother's head.

"I would like to thank you all for coming to see us this year in Tucson Valley. It's been an absolute joy to show you off to our friends and to spend quality time together. I look forward to spending good time with my grandkids when we get back to Illinois in a couple of weeks, but this place is very special to your dad and me, and to have you all here…" Mom wipes at her eyes.

Dad clears his throat. "Enough sap. Glad you're here and all of that, but let's eat your mother's lasagna before it gets cold. Cheers to safe travels and good health." He raises his wine glass. We follow suit. Hudson and Flynn raise their plastic cups.

"Here! Here!"

I glance at Ivy who is sleeping in the baby swing Mom had borrowed from Paula whose grandchildren visit often. Barley is sitting below her, snoring in rhythm to the classical music radiating from the swing.

"We are happy for your new job and life here in Tucson Valley, Rosi, but we are going to miss you in Illinois," Simon says as he takes a drink of his wine.

"Thanks, Simon. I'll let Mom and Dad spoil you exclusively for a bit before they come back to do the same with Barley and me."

"Deal."

As Mom dishes out slices of lasagna and conversation is flowing, Shelly's phone dings loudly. "Oh, shoot! Sorry!" She pulls out her phone to silence it, but something catches her eye.

"What is it, Shell?" asks Simon.

Shelly looks at me, wide-eyed.

"What's the matter?" I ask.

"It's a notification, one of those tabloid sites. But..." she looks at the boys who are shoveling bites of lasagna into their mouths. "Isn't Elena Templeton one of the performers in that show where one of...you know, one of those guys..." and she makes a line through the air under her chin with her finger.

"Yes. She performed as Star. Why?"

"Because there's just been a...ah...a...S-E-X tape released, starring her and some guy named JJ."

I look at her in surprise as Flynn starts singing, "S-E-X, S-E-X."

"Flynn!"

"What, Mommy?" he asks innocently. "S-E-X, yea, S-E-XXXXXXX," he sings louder.

"S-E-F-F-F-F-F," says Hudson.

Keaton throws his hand over his mouth so he doesn't laugh.

"What's that mean?" Mom asks.

"I'm not sure, but I wonder if this video is the reason for everything that happened that night."

"Can we at least get through one meal without talking about M-U-R-D-E-R?" asks Dad as he takes a bite of garlic bread.

"Mudder. Mudder," sings Flynn.

"How does he know what that spells?" Simon asks, his eyes growing with surprise.

"You, dear brother, have one gifted son."

Everyone breaks into laughter, the thoughts swirling in my mind put on pause.

Chapter 21

As soon as the boys have settled down for the night and we've said our goodbyes, Keaton and I drive together to the performing arts center. I'd filled Keaton in on my thoughts as we drove. The building is dark, and most of the community itself is likely heading to bed. I use my employee key and let us into the side door that Clyde Andrews had claimed he'd exited, though now we know he was otherwise detained in the bathroom. Not wanting to turn on the full lights of the auditorium, Keaton and I use our phones to shine a path up to the tiny storage closet aside the stage where Mario and I had found a pile of blankets and pillows. Keaton pulls the chain inside the closet to turn on the light. No more mice. Mario's thorough cleaning can be thanked for that.

"Leave it to Mario to be so neat," I say, spying the blankets carefully folded and placed on a shelf next to the floor cleaner. I touch the blankets, willing them to spill the secrets of what happened in this closet. My nails catch the edge of one of the blankets, a pattern of pawprints that have been torn in multiple spots. I wonder what was happening in this closet.

"What are you looking for?"

"I'm not sure."

"Mario has cleaned so well that there's no use in even mentioning this room to Officer Daniel. If I'd thought it held any clues, I should have told him a long time ago anyway."

"Do you think Elena met someone in the closet for a little rendezvous?"

"Rendezvous?" I ask, trying not to laugh.

"I'm trying to be polite."

"About a woman who made a sex tape?"

"I doubt she knew it'd be shared publicly. Again, I'm the only one here who's seen the whole footage." He raises his hand as if I'm supposed to high five him. "Even if Elena admitted to meeting someone in this closet for *relations*, it doesn't prove that she killed Sherman," says Keaton.

"No, it doesn't, but Elena's sex tape has to mean something."

"We know that Elena and JJ didn't release that video, right? Uh, from what I saw, it was less than flattering and wouldn't advance her career—even if they pivoted to the porn industry!" he laughs.

"Keats! You're terrible! But...but you're right. They wouldn't benefit from the video's release, or would they? Sex tapes *have* been known to forward a few careers."

"Not when there's a thirty year age difference between the...uh...subjects. Trust me. This is not a good look for Elena Templeton *or* JJ McMeadows," Keaton shudders.

"I think in this situation someone else had to have a motive to release that video, not to mention the ownership of the video itself. And I might know just the person."

It's nearly 10:30 when we pull into Dee's driveway, the Dee whose last name I never cared to learn. I'd taken her business card from my wallet and punched her address into my car's GPS while Keaton drove as I explained my theory. We can see the light from her television bouncing around through the large window at the front of her house, the only light in sight on this dark street.

"I still don't completely understand what you're doing here," Keaton says as he squeezes my hand before we get out of the car.

"I guess I just have a hunch. Do you trust me?"

"Trust your judgment? Well, you chose me, so I guess I have to," he smiles.

"Come on."

A motion sensing light turns on as we walk up the sidewalk. The lights from the television inside the house stop. I knock on the door. We see Dee peek through the curtains. I knock again. Slowly, the front door opens, a chain remaining in place for her protection. "Excuse me, Dee? I'm Rosi Laruee. We met at the Tucson Valley Retirement Community Performing Arts Center."

"Yes?" she says timidly, her red hair pulled back in a single braid.

"I'm so sorry to bother you this late. I was working tonight and realized that I still had Sherman Padowski's paycheck. I gave it some thought. You're right. I should give it to you to pass along to his family. After all, you were his assistant, correct?"

"Oh, yes. That would be great. I remember you. Thank you."

I pull out the envelope with Sherman's paycheck, a small price to pay for information, even if the performing arts center has to pay Sherman's family again because Dee pockets the money. She reaches below the chain for the check. I keep it just out of her reach. "I do have a question for you first, however, something that's been on my mind."

Dee unlatches the chain and opens the door a crack so that we are now face-to-face with Keaton off to the side, letting me do my thing. "I'd like to know why you released Elena Templeton and JJ McMeadows's sex tape."

As expected, Dee's face drains of color, and her eyes grow big. "I don't know what you're talking about."

"I think you do. I'd corresponded with a Dee who was JJ's assistant via email before the show with requests for his dressing room. Does manuka honey ring a bell?"

"Manuka…?"

"And then JJ told me you were no longer his assistant, that he'd fired you. Then you showed up claiming to be Sherman Padowski's assistant, trying not only to make a little money," I wave the check in the air, "but also to get more information about Sherman's death. Because you were sure that JJ or Elena had something to do with Sherman's death. Am I right?"

"Sherman was a good man. He gave me a job the second I asked, felt important because someone wanted to be *his* assistant. Made him feel like a bigshot. I didn't kill Sherman," Dee says softly, her eyes falling to her teddy bear slippers, an odd choice for a night in Arizona, though I can feel the air conditioning pumping from her home.

"Of course you didn't. You were home the night of the murder. But you must have some evidence to suggest that JJ or Elena had something to do with Sherman's murder—or you wouldn't have released the sex video."

Dee sighs. And sighs again. She looks from me to Keaton and back to me. "Is he a cop?" she asks, pointing at Keaton.

"No. He's a landscaper."

"I wasn't just JJ's assistant. That man had *needs, so many needs.* It wasn't just lavender candles and stupid jars of honey he wanted. And he told me I was the best assistant he'd ever had. I believed him, too—until the day I was cleaning his office and came across a file on his computer marked *Elena*. And I clicked it. He fired me when I confronted him but not before I'd downloaded the video."

"How did Sherman end up with the video?"

"I gave it to him. Why else do you think I became Sherman's assistant?"

"Why?"

"Elena is careless with her social media. She was talking up the Tucson Valley show, and in a couple of videos Sherman was in the background. Let's just say that she has a reputation for throwing herself at her fellow performers. And she was trying to make JJ jealous—even though she ended things. She's evil like that. She knew that JJ would be at the Tucson Valley show, too. I wanted to protect JJ, expose that harlot for who she really is."

"But JJ was in the video, too," I say confused.

"Of course he was. But just as I'd predicted with that video release, tons of men are going public with their own *stories* about Ms. Templeton, if you know what I mean," she says, cocking her head to the side.

I don't have the heart to tell Dee that JJ seems unfazed as he's still spending time with his *sweetie*. "How did you know that Sherman would release the video?"

"I wanted Sherman to release the video and show the world what a slut she is, sleeping with old men like that." She shakes her head back and forth. "And I knew that when Sherman saw Elena flirting with JJ during rehearsals, that he might just be angry enough to release the video."

"Why did she and JJ part ways?"

"Oh, that. JJ was crushed. I knew I was only a rebound, but I could have made that man happy if he could have gotten that tart out of his mind. She, on the other hand, doesn't care about anyone but herself."

"Are you suggesting that Sherman wanted a romantic relationship with Ms. Templeton?" I ask.

She laughs. "That's what Sherman thought, but he was gullible like that, thinking that woman wanted someone like him. She was only trying to seduce him to get the video back after she found out he had it."

"By throwing herself at him?"

"A girl's gotta do what a girl's gotta do, honey."

"Can I have that check now? Shermy would have wanted me to have it." She smiles up at the sky as if getting permission from the heavens.

"Why didn't *you* release the video earlier, Dee, if you wanted to embarrass Elena and make JJ reconsider his feelings for her?"

Dee dismisses my question with a wave of her hand. "Because I wanted clean hands," she says. "Clean hands. But then Shermy died, and I had to do what I had to do," she says sadly.

"Do you think that JJ and Elena killed Sherman to get the video back?"

She laughs so hard *my* stomach hurts. "Do you honestly think that a man who needs manuka honey for his throat and lavender candles to relax could kill someone?"

"And Elena?"

"Elena isn't the type to get her hands dirty, either. I'd look at her brother if I were you."

"Her brother?"

She laughs again, the kind of laugh meant to embarrass with judgment. "Xander Nolan. That's Elena's brother."

I hand Sherman's check to Dee and walk silently back to my car, Keaton following.

Chapter 22

Xander lives in a single-family home that looks like many of the small homes in Tucson, adobe brick exterior, a dull brown that matches the barren yard as well. There are bars on the windows which appear to be common in this neighborhood. Officer Daniel has been driving, and I've counted eight homes with bars on the windows and doors. Xander doesn't know we are coming, and we are both hoping he's home and this isn't a wasted trip. Keaton had wanted to come with us today, but I didn't think Dan's fragile ego could take it. He'd gone to work instead with my assurances that I'd call him if I learned anything important.

Dan knocks on the door. Today he's wearing his uniform, official business. He knocks a second time.

The door opens. Xander peeks around the heavy door and through the bars on the screen door. "Yes?" he asks, not clearly registering who is at his door.

"Hello, Mr. Nolan. Good to see you again. I'm Officer Daniel from Tucson Valley, and this is…"

"Rosi?" he asks, opening the door fully. "What are you guys doing here?"

"We were hoping we could ask you a few questions," says Officer Daniel.

"About what?"

"About Sherman Padowski and his relationship with your sister."

"My...sister?" he asks, his acting as paltry as his singing. I wonder if he'd even sung in public before the night of the 60s concert.

"Can we come in, Mr. Nolan?"

Xander looks behind him, assessing his home and whether or not it's good enough for an unexpected visit.

"Okay. But I have a lot of cats if that's a problem."

The first problem I can gather from all of the cats is the overwhelming stench of cat urine. A tabby cat sits on a tattered blanket on the back of an easy chair that partially covers the threadbare upholstery while a pair of black cats sit on matching blankets on each arm of the couch. A cat that may have been gray runs with full speed down the hallway when it sees us, while a beautiful, long-haired white cat curls its tail around Dan's leg. I choose to remain standing.

"Can you tell us why you and Elena kept your family relationship a secret?" I ask.

Xander sits on the edge of the couch, pushing off one of the cats. "It was her idea. She told me it would be better to keep it quiet. Sunny and Star were a married couple. Wouldn't it have been weird if the audience knew we were brother and sister?"

"I guess. I can understand that."

Xander smiles, almost as if he's relieved to hear this. I spy a pile of headshots sitting on the coffee table. "Are you using those for your next show?" I ask.

"My next show? I'm not doing another show. This was a one and done thing, only helping my sister out."

"Helping her out?" Dan asks.

Xander nervously crosses and uncrosses his legs. "Yeah, her normal Sunny Moon got sick last minute. That's why I stepped in."

"She didn't mention a sick partner," I say. "Your name was the only one I was ever given as the Sunny Moon impersonator."

"Yeah, he's actually been sick for a while."

"That's too bad."

"Yeah, nice guy, too."

"His name?" asks Officer Daniel, pulling out his notepad.

"His name?" Xander repeats.

"Uh, I'm not sure. I didn't really follow my sister's shows. Don't tell her I said that, though. I'm more of a sports guy, boxing and karate, that kind of thing."

"And can you tell us again what you were doing right after the show?" asks Officer Daniel.

"Yeah. I changed into a clean shirt after the show and signed autographs for fans. It was really fun—though I don't have the desire to do it again."

"Do you know anything about your sister's relationship with Mr. Padowski?"

"Sherman and my sister? Nah. I don't know anything about that."

"What about your sister and JJ McMeadows?" I ask.

"That old guy?" He shakes his head. "I don't know anything about that. I try to keep out of my sister's business. It only gets me into trouble when I get too involved."

"What do you mean?" I ask.

"Oh, I don't mean anything," he laughs nervously. "Silly sibling stuff, you know?"

"I suppose I can relate to that," I say.

"Mr. Nolan, if you can think of anything else that might be helpful, please reach out." He hands Officer Daniel his police business card.

"Will do."

"What do you make of what he had to say?" I ask when we are back in the car.

"He's hiding something."

"And I know what that is," I say more confidently than I feel on the inside.

Officer Daniel pulls his car over to the side of the road. "What are you talking about, Rosi?"

"The blankets," I say.

"The blankets?"

"There were three blankets covering Xander's furniture. An identical blanket, that looks like it's been shredded—by a cat—is sitting on a shelf in a tiny storage room next to the stage, right by where Sherman was pushed off the stage."

"And *WHY DON'T I KNOW ABOUT THIS ROOM?*"

"Because we weren't sure until recently that it meant anything. Mario and I found some leftover food from what I'd provided on Saturday and some blankets and pillows on the floor."

"Someone was napping in a closet?" Dan wrinkles his forehead and rubs his temples.

"Not napping."

"Then what was Xander doing in the closet and with whom?"

"Not Xander."

"Get on with it, Rosi," he says, frustrated with his failure to connect the dots that seem so clear to me.

"Remember that note we found in Elena and Nancy's trash can the night of the show?"

"The note about meeting someone somewhere, right?" he asks, seeking my approval as if *I* am the one leading this investigation.

"Yes, that's the one. I believe that Elena asked Sherman to meet her in the closet. Nancy had already seen them, uh, getting frisky in their dressing room. She needed a safe spot to meet him, a safe spot to lure him."

"I didn't get the impression from Nancy that Sherman needed any convincing to hook up with Ms. Templeton."

"That's very true, but Elena needed a way to get Sherman alone. She knew he had the sex video of her and JJ. She knew because Dee told us so. She wanted to seduce Sherman to stop him from releasing the video. And he wanted her to stop flirting with JJ. I'm sure he was livid when he found out their dressing rooms were so close, as requested by JJ."

"And when that didn't work, she asked her brother to kill him onstage at the end of the show? That seems like a stretch, Rosi."

"I don't think it's a stretch. Xander's blanket was in that room—just like the ones in his house. Xander set up the love lair for Elena to lure Sherman into. But Elena wasn't waiting for him. It was Xander. After the show he said he went back to the dressing room to change, which is true. But he only changed after killing Sherman and getting wine splashed all over his shirt. He used Clyde's bottle of wine to make you suspicious of Clyde since the two of them had been fighting all weekend. Nobody knew his connection with Elena. Do you think you can subpoena the phone records of Xander and Elena?"

"I can."

"Good. I think you'll probably find conversations to back up my theory. They were on their phones constantly."

"Huh," Officer Daniel says, relaxing his grip on the steering wheel. How surprised Elena and JJ must have been when the video was released anyway."

"Yeah, they didn't factor in another woman scorned. Dee is one woman I hope to never meet again. And if you can get the siblings to flip on each other for a deal, you might not even need those phone records."

"Huh," he says again. "Do you think JJ knew?"

"I have no idea. I think he was just heartsick over Elena and their past relationship. He wanted to protect her. He knew the video would embarrass Elena. She was desperate to stop Sherman from releasing it, so she pretended to care for him, and when that didn't work…well…"

"She had him killed."

"Yes."

"Then why do you think she's seeing JJ again? I think we interrupted something in the casino."

"Who knows? Maybe with the tape's release she thought it would look less embarrassing if she acted like she really cared for JJ, that they were a real couple. But I don't think she really cares about him. She doesn't seem like the type to care about anyone but herself."

"Poor JJ," Dan says as he shakes his head.

"Don't feel too sorry for him. He's still a prima donna."

Chapter 23

I'm back at my parents' house this morning after saying goodbye to Simon, Shelly, and the kids. Knowing that the whole family will be together in Illinois while I've chosen to start my life over thousands of miles from home might be tough although having Barley and a new condo to decorate will be fun distractions—and, of course, there's Keaton. He's pretty fun, too. And Simon is coming back in late fall when Mom and Dad return. He's agreed to have his company, the maker of the senior helper app, sponsor a Tucson Valley talent show to benefit the local homeless shelter. I'd introduced him to Kenny and explained the plight of some of the local residents. It'd been an obvious decision. Plus, the chance to see Mom and Tracy do a tap-dance routine will make our year.

The first sign that something is happening comes from the incessant dinging of Mom's phone. I'd be lying if I said that I didn't hope to hear the reliable dings of gossip today since Officer Daniel hasn't yet called. I think he's been holding any news to himself a bit longer so he feels as if he is in control of the narrative because once the news is out, it pivots and changes much as in a game of telephone. He can't blame himself, though, for the news getting out now. There are office staff at the police station that direct call their best friends the moment something exciting happens. And from there, the news flies down the lines of communication to the gossipy gaggles in the Tucson Valley Retirement Community.

Mom walks into the living room where Dad and I are watching the Sunday morning news. Barley is sitting on Dad's lap, reclaiming his spot from baby Ivy. "They've arrested a suspect for Filly Sinclair's murder," Mom says excitedly.

"I think you mean Sherman Padowski's murder," I correct her.

"Yes, of course. That was Jan."

"I assumed."

"Quiet. Here comes the story." Dad turns up the television.

Elena Nolan and Xander Nolan have been arrested for the murder of Sherman Padowski, the duo of impersonators, Sunny Moon and Star, during the Tucson Valley Retirement Community's Sizzling 60s performance on April 7th. Ms. Nolan, using the stage name of Elena Templeton, is accused of hiring her brother, Xander Nolan, to kill Sherman Padowski, a Filly Sinclair impersonator. Details about the motive have not yet been released.

"Did you know about this?" Mom asks.

"I did."

"What's this secret motive?"

I tell my parents about Elena and JJ's sex tape and how Sherman was threatening to release it if she didn't return his affections; and when he wouldn't give it to her, she'd had him killed. Only no one anticipated another scorned lover releasing the video anyway.

"My goodness," Mom says, clutching her chest. "We are going to miss so much while we are back in Illinois."

"Well, I hope there aren't any more murders," I say. "Are things always this exciting?"

"Nope, usually just golf and more golf for this guy," Mom says, pointing at Dad.

"And gossip and more gossip from this gal," Dad says, pointing at Mom.

"I'm really going to miss you guys."

"We're going to miss your fortieth birthday, Rosi!" Mom says sadly.

I give Mom a little squeeze. "We'll celebrate in a few months. I'm not going anywhere."

Mom gives me a kiss on the cheek, and I tuck this memory away, realizing that no matter how old I get, I'm still that little girl who wants her parents' love. And I know I have it.

The Tucson Valley Retirement Community Cozy Mystery Series:

Dying to Go (Nothing to Gush About)

Thirty-nine-year-old Rosi Laruee—named Rosisophia Doroche after her mother's beloved Golden Girls—decides that the end of her twenty-year marriage and her dad's impending knee replacement surgery are all the excuses she needs to visit Tucson Valley Retirement Community. But the drama follows Rosi when she finds the body of local tart and business owner, Salem Mansfield. The information she discovers using her newspaper reporter sleuthing skills coupled with the clues she picks up from lackluster Police Officer Dan Daniel lead to a surprise discovery when the murderer is revealed. Along the way, she meets a cast of characters in her parents' social circle who leave her questioning her parents' choices in friends while simultaneously befriending many of the residents, including a handsome landscaper and a brand-new Golden Retriever puppy she names Barley. Rosi's visit to Tucson Valley proves more than she'd bargained for, but maybe, she realizes, it's just the kind of change she needs. Laugh out loud with Rosi, and be prepared to get the happy feels along the way!

Dying for Wine (Seeing Red)

There's a rockin' concert of 1960s impersonators coming to Tucson Valley to perform in the snowbird send-off concert at the Tucson Valley Retirement Community Performing Arts Center. And as the one in charge, Rosi Laruee is thriving in the chaos. Diva attitudes, outrageous requests, and late flights don't sideline what is meant to be the greatest concert this community has ever seen. That is, until a dead body shows up below the stage next to the front row of seats. Now, she's sleuthing again with Officer Dan Daniel. Only this time, the murder is personal, and she needs to restore the reputation of Tucson Valley as being a safe place by solving this mystery quickly. What she discovers is a much deeper web of connections than she could have imagined. Throw in a condo search, a budding relationship with Keaton, and a growing Golden Retriever to Rosi's crazy adventures, and you have a recipe for hours of laughter.

Dying for Dirt (All Soaped Up)

Dying to Build (Nailed It)

Dying to Dance (Cha-Cha-Ahhh)

The Secret of Blue Lake (1)

The only true certainty in life is dying, but there's a whole lot of life to live from beginning to end if you're lucky. When Chicago news reporter Meg Popkin's dad makes a surprise move to a tiny town called Blue Lake, Michigan, in the middle of nowhere and away from his family after losing his wife to cancer, she wonders if there is more to the move than *just a change of scenery*. With the help of a new, self-confident reporter at the station, Brian Welter, she tries to figure out what the secret attraction to Blue Lake is for its many new residents and along the way discovers that maybe she's been missing out on some of the joys of living herself.

Drama, mystery, and romance abound for Meg as she learns about love, loss, and herself.

The Secret of Silver Beach (2)

After solving the mystery of the secret of Blue Lake, Meg returns to Chicago and to her new job as co-host on Chicago Midday. But when poor chemistry with Trenton Dealy leads to problems on the show, Meg is assigned a travel segment that will send her on location all around Lake Michigan visiting beach towns and local tourist attractions. The trip takes her away from fiancé Brian who has to continue anchoring the nightly news in Chicago. When odd threats start hurtling in Meg's direction, she finally confesses to Brian and those closest to her that she might have a stalker. Do the threats have something to do with the new information she learned about her dad's past in the little town of St. Joseph, Michigan, or is there something bigger at play that threatens more than Meg's livelihood?

The Secret of Blue Lake:
Chapter 1

"There's a pile up on the Dan Ryan," says my boss Jerry Stanley, his excitement for the craziest of news stories on full display. "A milk tanker collided with a truck carrying cocoa powder." He laughs, a deep hearty laugh that fills the newsroom. "I can't make this stuff up."

"Headlines writing themselves, huh?" I shake my head. It's never a dull moment at WDOU.

"Chocolate Milk Causes Road Closure on Busy Chicago Interstate," he says, smiling.

"Take a crew and talk to some people if you can—witnesses and drivers."

"Are there any fatalities?" It's the worst part of my job. Covering deaths is never easy, but since Mom died it's nearly impossible.

"No fatalities, Meg." He pats me on the shoulder. "Now get going. Take Brian with you. He needs to learn his way around Chicago," says Jerry.

I roll my eyes. The last thing I want to do is take our newest reporter Brian Welter *anywhere*. Before I can protest, I feel Brian's presence, his stale hidden-but-not-hidden cigarette stench permeating from his suit jacket. "Meggin Popkin!" He slaps the wall outside Jerry's office. "I hear I'm hanging with the number one street reporter."

I groan. No one calls me *Meggin* anymore. In a world full of Jennifers, Michelles, and Kristis, my parents bucked the trend and named their second child Megan, a different but regular-enough sounding name that they spelled M-E-G-G-I-N. I can appreciate their quest for originality, but with everyone spelling my name wrong, it was simpler to call myself Meg.

"Earth to Meggin!" Brian shouts through his cupped hands. No one should be allowed to yell at another person so closely unless in the throes of passion.

I wince at the sound of his annoying voice, ignore him, and head to my cubicle. He follows, landing in step with me. The news station abounds with energy and business, always with something going on in the Chicagoland area: the sounds of fingers on keys punching out stories or answering emails, the police scanners blaring, waiting to point a reporter to a new crime to cover, and the faint sound of elevator music playing through the overhead speakers that aim to calm the anxieties of the stories covered here.

"I'll meet you by the station van," I say. "I need to grab my phone."

"It's okay. I can wait for you. We can share an elevator. Go ahead and fix your hair, too, of course."

I know he's smiling a nauseating grin without even seeing his face. I've met this kind. I almost married this kind once before when I was young and dumb. Now I know better. But I don't get asked my opinion about new on-air talent. Even though Brian Welter comes with accolades galore for his on-air presence in Tucson, his *in-person* presence is nothing short of arrogance.

I ignore Brian as I grab my jacket along with my phone while shutting down my laptop. I have a superstition about leaving my computer on when I'm not at my desk. I don't want anyone seeing a story before it's buffed up and ready for its audience.

Brian stands to the side of the hallway as I brush past him. He rushes by to push the elevator button like a little boy fighting with his sister over who gets to push all the buttons. When Lara and I were little, we'd been assigned days. I got to do the "things" on even-numbered days while Lara got to do them on the odd-numbered days. Mom said that system cut our arguments in half. Something tells me Brian was an only child who never learned the value of compromising or perhaps the oldest who always thinks he's right. I can't help but glance in the elevator mirror before the door opens, making sure my bangs are aligned and no strands of my shoulder-length brown hair have parted on their own accord. Satisfied, I slide out the door before Brian.

Brian reaches the station van first and grabs the passenger seat door handle before I can stop him.

"No, you don't," I say, slapping my hand on the door handle, too.

"There's not room for both of us, kid." He brushes my hand away as he slips into the van.

"What an ass." I slam the backseat door.

"You'd better not mess with Meg, man," says Tom. We make eye contact through the rearview mirror. You don't make friends at a news station by ruffling the feathers of the cameraman.

"*Her?* I think I can handle *Meggin*," he says, laughing.

"I don't need *handling*. Drive, Tom." Tom accelerates so quickly that Brian's phone slides off the dashboard and crashes into the door.

"Dammit, Tom!" he says as he reaches for his phone.

Tom, our cameraman, has been recording my news segments since I first came to WDOU five years ago. Tom and I are more than work associates. We are friends. He and his wife, Anita, were the first people in line at Mom's visitation when she died. He still brings me leftovers once a week, either extra meat he'd grilled with a side of potatoes or an extra portion of stir fry. Tom cares for me like a little sister. I know he's got my back.

I put in my AirPods before I can hear more of Brian's drivel. I watch the busy city streets pass by as we race to the scene of the chocolate milk interstate. It's easy to imagine myself living on one of those little side streets living the life of a school librarian like I'd grown up thinking I'd be. Walking the stacks, looking for the perfect alphabetical placement, sneaking in readings of newly published books. There are days when I wished I'd never gone with Dad to his job at the newspaper, when management had called for a reporter to cover the local school board meeting, and he'd looked at me and asked his boss to let me go because no one wanted the gig. And I'd gone. And I'd fallen in love with telling stories, stories of boring school board meetings to stories of convenience store break-ins to stories of interstate pileups. But some days I still wonder what it would be like living the privacy of a librarian's job without being critiqued for every outfit choice or inadvertent nose booger.

Tom grabs his camera after finally finding a place to park in a back alley between Garfield and S. Wentworth Avenue. We take the chance of getting towed, and it wouldn't be the first time. The station budgets for such expenses. *Get to the story first. Worry about the van second.*

It's a hike up the embankment to the interstate. No one should get twenty feet within distance of a Chicago interstate under normal circumstances, the cars flying miles over the speed limit, weaving in and out of traffic. But no one is moving today. I count fifteen cars that have experienced some bit of fender or bumper damage, the highway beneath our feet a cloudy brown color mixing the cocoa powder from one over-turned semi-trailer with the milk of another. I toss a glance at the side streets below the interstate and wonder again why I'm not living the life of a single librarian. It might not seem glamorous, but to me it sounds perfect right about now. The early spring temperatures in Chicago make me shiver involuntarily. I hope the chocolate milk washes away the dirty snow that lines the road. Only the first winter snow in Chicago is welcome. Every snow after lingers as a mess of dirt and trash and pollution alongside the streets for months until the temperatures warm up long enough for fresh rains to wash it away.

"Meg, you have a perspective yet?" asks Tom. He rests a camera on his shoulder and points at the scene before us, a mess of banged up-cars and trucks with people on their phones and milling around the scene talking with police and other emergency workers.

"Yeah, sorry. I'll start with that blue car. It's the closest one to the cocoa powder truck." I point to a large white truck with pictures of chocolate bars on the side. I remember that I haven't eaten lunch today. The truck is on its side, the back half blocking the right lane of traffic and the back door swung open with punctured containers of cocoa powder spilling out. The milk truck it collided with is also on its side, in the adjoining left lane with its back door open, too. Milk continues to drip down and out the truck and into the cocoa powder below.

Tom starts to follow me as I weave between cars heading to the young woman who is leaning against her car and talking on the phone. Her compact car rests against the side of the road with a bumper that looks like a large accordion after making what looks like impact with the back tire of the cocoa powder truck.

I flash my station credentials in front of her. She drops the phone to her side.

"Excuse me, miss. I'm Meg Popkin with WDOU. I'd like to ask you a few questions."

She looks at Tom who is directing his camera at her. "Okay. I can talk," she says, brushing her hands through her long brown hair, a not-so-subtle attempt to be camera ready. "I…I've been crying," she says as she looks at the camera.

I smile reassuringly. "I imagine you have. It's been a scary day."

She smiles, too, comforted by the first in-person contact she's had since the accident. "I'm Quinn," she says.

Quinn answers my questions, becoming visibly calmer as I finish learning about the accident and its effect on her. She'd been talking to her boyfriend on the phone—hands free, of course—when the collision had occurred from behind, sending her sliding into the back of the semi-truck. She's relaxed enough to laugh about the absurdity of the mess that covers the interstate. "I guess all we need now are some cookies," she says amused with her own wit.

I thank her for her time and turn to leave when Brian grabs the microphone from my hand. I hadn't even noticed he was standing behind me. "What the...?" I ask.

"Quinn, when will you be filing your lawsuit?" he asks, thrusting the microphone so close to Quinn's face it nearly knocks out a tooth.

"A what?" She wrinkles her nose and looks at me.

"Give me back my microphone," I say, trying to yank it from Brian's firm grip.

He pulls it away and back into Quinn's face. "A lawsuit," he repeats. "You stand to make a lot of money from this accident, you know?"

"I...I don't want money. I want my car fixed and to move on. This has been the scariest day of my life." She looks at me, any sense of calmness disappearing from her face.

"Shut off the camera," I say to Tom. He glances at Brian who is giving him a stink eye while shaking his head back and forth. "Shut it off, Tom," I repeat.

Tom nods his head and pulls the camera from his shoulder. He knows who the boss is here. "Thanks, Quinn. Sorry about my associate. Best wishes to you." I walk away. Tom follows.

After speaking with the driver of the milk truck and another driver who'd witnessed the collision, I'm still angry with Brian. I stomp through the chocolate milk and dirty snow back to the embankment. I sidestep my way down the hill but lose my footing on a slippery patch of snow and finish my trek down the hill on my butt. I try to stand up right away, but I slip again, this time falling forward. My pants are soaking wet. My hands are muddy, and I've lost a shoe. My day keeps getting better.

Brian arrives first at the scene of *my accident* which surprises me since he'd left my shadow after trying to mess up my interview with Quinn, his reporter's notebook hanging out of his back pocket. He doesn't hold in his laughter as he jogs down the hill behind me. "You really know how to make an exit," he says. "Here, grab my hand." He reaches his hand out to me.

I slap it away and accept Tom's help when he's rejoined us after filming more images but not shots with Brian in them. "Are you okay, Meg?" he asks, pulling me to my feet.

"I'm fine," I say too cheerily, "Nothing damaged!"

"But how's your ego?" Brian asks as he hands me my shoe.

"My *ego* is solid though not as large as yours." I stomp through the dirty snow as quickly as I can to get back to the van first and grab hold of the passenger door.

Tom throws me an old towel for the front seat, and I slam the door shut behind me before Brian can reply. Still, I have to give it to Brian to find another way to get the story even when the cameraman had taken my side for the day. We don't talk all the way back to the station.

"Send the tape to editing," Jerry says when I walk into the station. "We're going to run it on the 5:30 news. What took you guys so long?" he asks before seeing my muddy clothes. "What happened to you, Meg?" His eyes are as big as teacup saucers. Jerry is a great boss. Part of being a great boss it making sure things are done right and on time. And *without incident,* his favorite phrase when out on assignment.

"She bruised her bum, apparently, but not her ego, Jerry. This one's a tough cookie," Brian says gleefully.

I glare at him.

"Jerry, I have the best stories to tell," says Brian.

I purse my lips and stare at Brian. He's smiling so widely that his perfect teeth look like they'll pop out of his mouth with one swing.

"You went on camera?" Jerry asks, raising an eyebrow in surprise and ignoring my appearance for a moment.

"Well, actually I like to talk to my sources *off camera* first. Then I record my reflections on camera when I get back to the station. The camera intimidates sources from talking when they've been through something traumatic," he says, smiling as fake as the eyelashes on a Hollywood starlet.

I want to vomit from the acridness of his words. Plus, I really want to clean up and change clothes.

"So, I think I'll use the stationary camera I saw in the back offices to record my segment for tonight's news."

"That is ridiculous!" I can't hold back. "Jerry, I have a witness on camera who gave me an awesome interview. I talked to the driver of the milk truck. That's all we need along with Tom's shots of the scene. This isn't a major story, after all. We don't need Brian to do *anything*."

Jerry looks between Brian and me. I know he's weighing his options—keeping me happy and accommodating the new guy. "Hmm…Brian, go ahead and record your piece. Meg, take Brian's segment to editing with your segment." He sighs and curses under his breath. "You know I'm not happy about this. It's going to put us right up to news time. You are both making my job harder. If you learn to play nicely, things will be a lot easier for *all* of us." He walks away a few steps before adding. "You have 45 minutes. No exception. And clean yourself up, Meg! You look a mess!"

I death stare at Brian who has the audacity to laugh out loud. "If you play nice, you get what you want. You heard Jerry, Meg. Seems like you need to learn how to be nice. Grab a drink with me tonight, and I'll teach you how to be nice." He winks at me.

"I'd rather drink alone for the rest of my life than ever go out with you."

He snorts out loud and covers his mouth with a sickening giggle. "*That,* my dear, is not a stretch to imagine. Enjoy your solitude."

"You have fifteen minutes to get your part to me or the editing department won't have time to mesh it with mine!" I spit out before Brian saunters away.

I watch him walk away to record his story—my story—and dream about taking off my low black pump and throwing it at his head.

War and Me   By: Marcy Blesy

Amazon Reviewer: *The story and characters draw you in. I felt like I was in the story and feeling the emotions of each character. I laughed. I cried. I couldn't put the book down! The story takes place during the WW2 era and intertwines love with the realities of war. A must read!*

Flying model airplanes isn't cool, not for fifteen-year-old girls in the 1940's. No one understands Julianna's love of flying model airplanes but her dad. When he leaves to fly bomber planes in Europe forcing Julianna to deal with her mother's growing depression alone, she feels abandoned until she meets Ben, the new boy in town. But when he signs up for the war, too, she has to consider whether letting her first love drift away would be far easier than waiting for the next casualties.

Marcy Blesy is the author of over thirty children and adult books including the popular children's series: Evie and the Volunteers, Niles and Bradford, Third Grade Outsider, Hazel, the Clinic Cat, and Be the Vet. Her picture book, Am I Like My Daddy?, helps children who have experienced the loss of a parent. Her adult books include cozy mysteries and romance books including the Tucson Valley Retirement Community Cozy Mystery Series. By day she teaches creative writing to wonderful students around the world.

Marcy is a believer in love and enjoys nothing more than making her readers feel a book more than simply reading it.

I would like to extend a heartfelt thanks to Betty for being the first person to read The Tucson Valley Retirement Community cozy mysteries and for giving me her guidance and expertise as my editor.

Thank you to Ed, Connor, and Luke for always championing my dreams and for believing in me. Thank you to Tom, Cheryl, and Megan for being such supports with my writing and in life.

And, finally, I'd like to think that my *Golden Girls* and *Murder She Wrote*-loving mom is smiling down on me, and perhaps, reading over my shoulder. Love you, Mom.

Made in United States
North Haven, CT
27 July 2024